WITHIN
SACRED
WALLS

NELL TORONE

PublishAmerica
Baltimore

First printing

ISBN: 1-59286-108-3
PUBLISHED BY PUBLISHAMERICA BOOK PUBLISHERS
www.publishamerica.com
Baltimore

Printed in the United States of America

This book is dedicated to my father, who always believed in me.

To my husband for his never-ending support and encouragement to follow my dreams.

Special thanks to all my family and friends that helped me along the way with words of inspiration.

PROLOGUE

January 1809, Charlestown, Massachusetts

A babe grew within her. Abigail Fraser smoothed her trembling hand over her flat stomach with amazement and sheer panic. Not just any child, she thought hysterically – Francis McBrien's child.

Her breath caught in her throat, thinking, worrying what to do. Sarah Perkins, the local mid-wife's apprentice, confirmed her suspicions and promised to keep the news quiet, but Abigail worried that she'd be arrested for her condition, put in chains or worse.

Waves of nausea churned up inside her as she strolled down the street towards St. Joseph's church, trying to look as if all was right with the world. She pulled the delicate handkerchief from her dark wool cape and wiped drops of moisture staining her forehead like tiny beads of guilt in the chilled morning air. Everything would be all right, she assured herself, as soon as she reached Francis. He'd make her laugh, smooth out her knots of worry, and show her how foolish she had been. Her heart lightened at the thought.

She followed along the narrow stone path off the road toward St. Joseph's church, where Francis – no, rather Father McBrien – would be. Mustn't forget to address him by his new title, she scolded herself.

The church, framed in fieldstones, was set back from the road, nestled in a grove of tall pine trees. Two long arched windows sat on each side of the thick wood front doors.

She stopped a moment in front of the glass pane and did her best to smooth back strands of hair that came loose from her knot of disorderly blond hair. She pinched her cheeks for color and smoothed her hands down the length of her long gray cotton dress – standard attire of the academy.

When her body moved toward the door, a swell of nausea overwhelmed her, making her struggle to gain breath. She braced a hand against the stone wall of the church, body bent at the waist, and willed in slow steady breaths of air. She fought the urge to run – no, race – away from there.

She reminded herself that she had visited Francis on many occasions. Today would be no different. Then shook her head to clear it. Of course, *everything* would be different after this morning.

Candles flickered within the front entrance of the church as well as along the passage that led to where Francis would be working – alone.

There she found him, bent over his desk, reading text. She stood on the threshold of his door, watching him. Her hand unconsciously moved to her stomach.

Wisps of brown hair fell onto his forehead, giving him a rumpled young boy look, though she had proof growing inside her that he was all man. His body tall and lean with long legs cramped beneath his desk, his brows creased as he studied the book before him.

Her heart melted, as it always did, the minute his deep brown eyes turned toward her.

"What a wonderful surprise!" He jumped up to close the door behind her, pulling her close. "How did you know Father O'Connor would be away this afternoon? He only left minutes ago."

Tears lodged in her throat while she stood silently before him, her body stiff. His hands reached out to rub the length of her arms as he always did to calm her.

"What's troubling you, Abby? Is it the Superior? She can be harsh, but Father O'Connor says she is a fair woman."

Abigail shook her head. "I've news to tell you."

"Is it one of your aunts, then? Are they in poor health?" he asked concerned.

Again, she shook her head.

"Tell me, Abigail. We've a special bond, you and I. Now that I've become an official priest, I'll be your confessor," he encouraged with a wink, straightening his stiff new collar, his smile wide.

The way he wore his priesthood like a badge of honor made her heart sink. She wanted to be delighted for his achievement, his new role in society, instead she choked back tears threatening to fall.

Her eyes searched his for the answer before she gained the courage to speak the words. "I'm with child."

The air went still, and only the staunch beating of her heart drummed loudly in her ears.

"Are you certain?" he asked, his hands gripping her arms, his eyes a little wild at the edges.

At her nod, his hands abruptly released her. A splash of cold air washed over the length of her body when he strode across the room away from her.

She assured herself once the shock wore off, his mind would clear just as hers did, and he'd see the joy in the gift they were both given. He'd take care of her just like he promised on that lazy afternoon by the creek.

When he turned back toward her, his face had hardened. His eyes had lost all warmth. He cleared his throat and took on the tone of counselor. "Do you have any idea who fathered this child?"

Her eyes welled up with tears, her cheeks burned with embarrassment. "There has been no one but you," she replied into the quiet of the room, praying the painful ache in her heart would subside. She turned around to leave.

He took a step towards her, then hesitated, his fingers pinching the bridge of his nose. "I cannot be blamed for one transgression before I took my vow of celibacy. You can't do this to me after all I've acquired. God has placed me in this position. I'm needed here. I thought you understood that."

It was as if he had physically slapped her. "Do this to *you*? You didn't question your actions when you took away my innocence, did you? I am with child – *your child*," she stressed loudly, almost hysterically.

Suddenly, the door swung open behind them. Father O'Connor, senior pastor of St. Joseph's church, burst into the room, heaving in deep gulps of air, looking like he ran all the way from town. The normally gentle demeanor of the priest now looked hard and unbending – similar to Francis. His imposing form stepped toward her, towering over her small body, gripping his Bible like a weapon.

His eyes studied Francis's pale face, then swung to hers and back again. She blanched when his vindictive eyes leveled on her.

"Who is with child?" the elderly priest asked, his voice ringing with authority, commanding an answer.

7

Abigail raised her shame-filled eyes toward him. "I am."

His eyes shot back across the room like daggers sailing through the air, pinning Francis to the wall. "And who is the father?" he asked Francis, his voice deadly calm.

"I've no idea. Miss Fraser wouldn't tell me," Francis stuttered out, looking away. Never before had he looked so small, so petty.

Abigail choked back tears. What did she think would occur? This man, who had just taken sacred vows to devote his entire life to God, would give it all up for her? She opened her heart to him, trusted him with her every thought, and gave all that she had of herself, only to have him turn away from her as if he loathed the very sight of her.

"Abigail, it's only right to give us the name of the culprit that ruined you, so that we can make it right in the eyes of the Lord. Tell me his name," Father O'Connor demanded.

Her eyes swayed to Francis's averted face before she turned back to the elderly priest's face. "I cannot."

Her old room in the aunts' cottage should have given her comfort.

"Cry, scream, shout – do anything but stare at the ceiling!" Aunt Liddea instructed, losing her patience.

She had no desire to scream, grinding her teeth together against the next wave of pain that assaulted her. The punishment for her transgression she fully embraced, hoping then that the blanket of despair that hung on her like a heavy winter quilt would finally disappear. She'd endure any amount of pain to make it all go away, to bring her life back to the way it was, to finish her schooling at the nunnery.

Her stomach stiffened in pain, drenching her in nausea and sweat. She longed for the touch of her mother's comforting hand. If only the pain would end, she thought, her body rigid with agony.

Aunt Bea wiped her face with a cool cloth and squeezed her hand. "This babe can't make it out on his own. He needs your help. Push, child, as hard as ye can!"

She screamed until her lungs ached, straining to push as hard as she could. At the sound of a baby's cry, she dropped back limply onto the bed.

"Ye've born a son!" Aunt Liddea announced, holding the child up for her to see.

She closed her eyes to sleep, not wanting to view the babe, hoping she'd awake to it all being a dream.

It seemed like yesterday that Father O'Connor quietly arranged for her to leave the convent without a word to anyone, not even the Mother Superior.

No word came from Francis since the last time they spoke. Months of hopeful waiting for a letter or message of any kind telling her how wrong he had been. Now, whether he liked it or not, he had a son.

Sinful child, Father O'Connor had called her while Francis stood by silent, his face blank of emotion. If not for her aunts' kind hearts willing to take her back in, she would have been thrown onto the streets to fend for herself.

Aunt Bea patted her hand, interrupting her thoughts. "Abigail Fraser, ye did a fine job. This will be a new beginning for you and your child."

She was in no mood for a new beginning. She wanted things to be as they were before her stomach swelled to the size of a melon.

Days came and went. Instead of the sin being purged from her body, it lay like a heavy vice about her neck, squeezing the lifeblood out of her. There was only one way to make it disappear, prevent her transgression from spreading onto the innocent babe that cried endlessly into the night.

She walked into the tiny cove the aunts made into a nursery and found Aunt Bea rocking the babe swaddled in soft blankets.

"Abby, have ye come to hold your sweet babe?" Aunt Bea asked.

She nodded and gingerly took the crying babe into her arms and sat in the rocker. He settled into sleep, his tiny eyes closing with a yawn.

"He knows his mama," Aunt Bea quietly voiced before she tiptoed out of the room.

She hugged him close, nuzzling her nose against the satiny smooth skin of his sweet cherub face, memorizing the scent of him, all peaches and cream. She reveled in the boy that would someday become a man. Her fingers lightly rubbed the soft hairs on his head. What would he be, what would he do? Hopefully, he'd not make the same mistakes as her.

Softly, she whispered into his ear, "I love you," and wiped the few tears that slipped from her eyes with the back of her hand, then placed the sleeping child into his bed and walked out of the room.

Riding atop the horse with the wind blowing through her hair always improved her spirits. She rode to her favorite perch filled with flowers high on top a plateau overlooking a deep green valley.

She breathed in the sweet scent of heather with the sun setting behind the mountains, a melancholy smile on her face. This she would do for her son, the only way to make up for the disgrace she brought upon him.

Without hesitation, she took a step off the ledge into open air.

CHAPTER ONE

July 1834, Charlestown, Massachusetts
Curiosity anchored her eyes on the sinful image in front of her. She moved closer to her bedroom window, instinctively knowing she should look away but physically unable to do so.

In awe, she gaped at the man's towering physique and the length of his long, muscular legs planted firmly beneath him. Her eyes shifted to the thin worn material of his shirt, watching it stretch tightly over his broad shoulders as he swung the heavy mallet to set the fence post. His sweat-soaked shirt clung to his form, revealing the hard lines of his well-proportioned body. The russet brown of his hair hung in loose strands onto his shoulder, reminding her of the sleek mare stabled in the barn.

A soft gasp escaped her lips when she realized he had stopped working and turned around toward her, his eyes staring just as intently back at her. He stood stock-still, hands clasped over the newly set post, chin resting comfortably on top of them, a look of faint amusement on his face.

The Angelus bell rang for the start of morning prayers.

Startled, Brianna quickly turned away from the window with her hand pressed firmly against her racing heart. Her face flush with embarrassment, her breathing erratic. *Rules of St. Ursula Number Three – Never approach or look directly out the window of the Monastery.* Now she knew why!

She breathed in short pants, wheezing against the thick, smothering air of her bedroom and the frantic beating of her heart. Lightheaded, she hurried back to her bed.

This must certainly be her punishment for breaking yet another rule. Would she never learn to obey? Either she began to fit into this new way of life, or she'd be sent out into the real world to fend for herself. Hadn't Mother insinuated that after last week's escapade?

Lord, I would be forever grateful if you could make it clear to

Mother to allow me to stay within these walls.

She snuggled back under the starch white sheets of her narrow bed and tried to go back to sleep, maneuvering her feather pillow every which way to get comfortable. But the second her lids closed, the muscular form of the man working outside her room popped up before her eyes and made her feel even worse. Maybe a glass of water might quell her morning jitters and help her to forget the image of the man.

She hurried down the empty hall of the convent toward the kitchen. *Rules of St. Ursula Number Five – Never make noise while walking in the monastery.* Yes, she was very good at that. Smiling to herself, she thought how superbly she was doing *Rules of the Reverend Mother Number Six – Never lift our eyes while walking in the passageways.* Her heartbeat slowed to its normal pace, leaving her feeling more like herself until her body collided into something hard.

Her eyes skittered up from the finely polished oak planks of the floor to the huge hands that clasped her arms steadying her. Slowly, she lifted her eyes, with more courage than she thought she possessed, and stared straight into the deep brown eyes of the same man she was admiring only minutes ago. Her heart lodged in her throat.

"Skippin' yer prayers, are ye?" he chastised, his deep voice laced with the same Scottish lilt of all the hired hands.

As much as she tried to gain her voice, she couldn't do anything but gape at the size of the man that stood so uncomfortably close to her.

"I … I'm late … must go," she stuttered out, glancing down at the hands that branded her arms with the heat of their touch.

He leaned his devilishly handsome face close to hers, so close that she could smell the mint on his breath. He motioned his head in the opposite direction. "Chapel's that way."

Brianna closed her eyes and desperately tried to calm down, but the nearness of the stranger disconcerted her. She had never stood so close to any man. "Yes, well," were the only words she could think to say.

"Didn't mean to distract ye from your prayin'," he continued, hoping that his voice contained the right amount of honey to entice the young jittery nun into his confidence. He knew his nearness flustered her. Even used it to his advantage, purposely leaning forward, his breath a whisper in her ear. "I hope ye can forgive me startling ye, lass."

His hands still held lightly onto her arms, was her last thought before the world suddenly became dark.

This morning, she woke up in bed confused and couldn't figure out how she got there, *unless that man had....*

Brianna blinked away the discomforting thought, standing at the entrance of the chapel, decanter of holy water held firmly in her hands. She felt God's holy presence whispered into every corner of the room, from the dark mahogany pews to the floor, a golden honey, finely waxed and polished. The light streaming in from the arched stained glass windows sprayed rainbows of color on white walls.

Hastily, she began to fill each of the vessels at the entrance of the chapel, careful not to spill a single drop of holy water in her rush. Thoughts of what had occurred this morning kept causing her mind to wander. It was impossible to concentrate on the simple task at hand without making her already unsteady hand splash a few drops of the precious holy water, blessed by the bishop himself, onto the sanctuary floor. Quickly, she blocked out her anxious thoughts and hurried down the center aisle to the next vessel.

"Brianna, what's your rush, child?" Mother Superior demanded.

Brianna spun around and dropped to her knees before her Superior. When she glanced up the length of her long, flowing black robe, she found the Reverend Mother's stern face looking back down at her.

She sighed deeply, which only made her Superior's eyebrows arch down even further in disapproval.

"Permission to speak?" At her Superior's nod, she continued, "I'm late with my chores, and the bell for confession is about to ring."

"Slow your pace, Brianna. I'm sure that God would not want you to rush through such important tasks," she scolded.

"Yes, Mother. I'll remember that," Brianna replied, still kneeling, her head bowed low.

"And, Brianna, shine the ciborium after you're done filling the vessels in the sanctuary," her Superior stated casually as if the task wasn't the most privileged and honored chore she had ever been given.

As soon as the door of the chapel closed behind her Superior, Brianna moved down the center aisle toward the altar. She walked with decorum and grace, her footsteps measured and restrained. The honorable chore deserved no less.

She approached the altar, genuflecting low before the small crucifix that sat on top of a delicate lace cloth set in the center of the table. The ciborium was nestled in the mahogany tabernacle behind the holy table.

She opened the small wooden door of the tabernacle and with trembling hands pulled out the ciborium – the holiest of vessels. Using a soft cloth, her hand moved reverently over the silver exterior of the vessel that contained the consecrated bread, the holy body of Jesus Christ.

The honor of this new chore gave her renewed faith that the Reverend Mother would soon allow her to begin her journey as a nun.

When she felt that it sparkled sufficiently, she set it carefully back inside the tabernacle, then sat down on a pew to wait for the bell to ring.

With her eyes resting closed, she heard a deep voice whisper beside her ear. "We meet again."

She would have jumped out of her seat with fright if not for the man's heavy hand on her shoulder holding her there. She rose to leave, but his next words stopped her.

"Ye're hurtin' me feelin's, Miss. I'm beginnin' to think ye don't like my company."

She felt the blood drain from her face when thoughts of this morning came sailing back into her head. Her eyes stared at the huge arms that must have carried her back to her room.

Into the uncomfortable silence, he stated, "I didn't fancy nuns had idle time on their hands."

Then her eyes watched him kneel down to examine a raised peg,

14

hammering it flush with the wood plank of the floor. Her eyes mesmerized by his huge hands smoothing over the surface of the floor, searching for another wayward peg. His massive shoulders filling the space between them.

He arched his head around, caught her staring at his shoulders, and winked with a half grin that sent her pulses racing.

She was thankful that he swiveled back around before her breathing became impaired. She looked down, embarrassed at the fact that she was caught sitting with her legs stretched out beside her on the pew, definitely unbecoming of a future Ursuline nun.

Embarrassed and worried that he would report her indolence to the Reverend Mother, she blurted out the first thing that came to her mind. "I was praying … the rosary," she added to be more specific.

"Beggin' yer pardon, Miss, but yer hands are empty of beads," he pointed out plainly to her, his eyes glancing down to her empty hands.

She flushed profusely when she realized her mistake. "I … I've memorized it all," she finally blurted out.

With that said, she squeezed past his large frame that more than filled the small space between the pews and made her way to the center aisle. She held her head high even when she heard his light chuckle behind her.

When she questioned the Reverend Mother about the man, without mentioning, of course, that she had actually spoken without permission to this stranger, she was told that he would be doing repairs inside the building. He worked only at the specified times that all the sisters were in the chapel. Kindly ignore his presence, Reverend Mother told her, as if that was an easy thing to do.

Her day, she thought with a sigh, started out badly and was about to get worse. She hurried down the hall toward the confessional.

Upon entering the darkened room, lit by only one wax taper, she fought to slow the erratic beat of her heart, wishing she had little to nothing to confess, like her roommate Sister Mary Louise. Her knees bent to the floor beside the nuns to await the arrival of Reverend Mother.

She should be grateful that Mother gave her this opportunity to experience a nun's life rather than be sent from the convent, away from the only home she knew. The thought, unfortunately, did nothing to ease her apprehension. Instead, it made her feel worse, thinking of the number of rules she disobeyed this week, today especially.

Mentally, she checked off each rule broken as Sister Mary Margaret read aloud the rules of Saint Ursula – the patron Saint of the Ursuline nuns. Next, she prioritized her sins, as Mother had suggested to her last week, confessing only the sins that weighed heavily on her soul and that she wished to have absolved.

"Brianna?" Mother called.

On shaky legs, Brianna stepped forward and knelt before her Superior.

"Shortened version only, Brianna, in all fairness to the other sisters," her Superior softly whispered.

"Mother, I acknowledge that I have broken the rules of the Holy Order by neglecting to sprinkle my bed with holy water last night. It was not an intentional disobedience since I fell asleep before I could perform the task."

"Go on, Brianna," Mother encouraged.

"I know I am never to look directly out of the windows of the convent, Rules of St. Ursula Number Three, but I did, and the sight caused me to become ill." When she glanced up, she noticed her Superior's eyes widen slightly at the fact. She sighed and continued. "When rushing down the passageway, I ran into the man doing the repairs on the convent. I know Rules of St. Ursula Number Eight instructs never to touch anything without permission. But I couldn't help it, because my eyes were downcast while walking down the hallway, Rule Number Six, and didn't see the man until my body collided with his and … Irushedthroughmydutiesthismorning," she said in one breath, seeing her Superior's patience beginning to thin.

"A man?" Mother repeated.

"The man doing the repairs around the building," Brianna explained, then cleared her throat and said, "I most humbly ask a pardon of God, and of you, most Holy Mother."

"Brianna, your penance shall be the same as last week," Reverend Mother instructed her. Her hand did the sign of the cross in the air above Brianna's head.

"You may raise your eyes to see what lies in your path to avoid further mishaps," her Superior quietly advised.

Brianna bent down low to kiss the feet of her Superior before she hurried out of the room, grateful to be done with the chore.

His eyes scanned the storm clouds that cluttered the sky, matching his own brooding mood. It sickened him that he'd been obsessing over that nun's lustful green eyes all morning. He spent precious time inside the chapel, dallying at her side, like a young lad ogling a pretty girl, when he should have been focusing on the job at hand, coaxing information from her.

There were doors at the back of the chapel he didn't get to search, because he, the ace reporter known to get to the heart of any story, was too busy watching her slim form flutter about filling vessels inside the room. Rooms where punishment could be doled out.

He'd need to stay away from the nun. This story was too important to be distracted by a pretty face. No matter how much he longed to loosen the ribbon from her braided hair just to see it again pour like liquid fire down the length of her back.

When he nearly walked straight into the barn door, he knew it had been too long since he woke up to a warm woman snuggled up next to him in bed.

Tonight, he'd find himself a woman, a *real* woman, not one closeted in a building under the guise of religion, and he'd erase the feel of that nun's slender body from his memory forever.

His frustration grew when he turned to see Henry Snead walk out of the dark shadows of the barn. Quickly, Shawn moved to the barn door and shut it firmly behind them. The short, cocky man he called boss stood with his black eyes slightly crossed, dark hair oiled back, and a permanent sneer on his cigar-filled mouth.

"What the hell are ye doin' here, Snead? Do ye want to blow my cover?" Shawn asked, irritated.

Snead pulled the cigar from his mouth, tapping the ashes onto the dirt floor of the shed. "Got anything yet?"

"Ye'll have yer story right after I finish writing it. I'm no going to report every moment of me time here to ye. That's not the way I work," Shawn replied. He strode to the barn door, cracked it open, and looked out.

"No story, no pay," his boss reminded him, sticking the cigar back into his crooked mouth.

"I'm not in this for the money, as ye well know," Shawn flatly stated with disgust.

"Whatever the reason, I'm here to check on your progress. I took a risk hiring a newcomer. Came to make sure the job is done right," Snead explained.

"Don't patronize me, Snead. Ye know I'm the best reporter ye ever had or ever will have. I'd never work for slime the likes of ye, if not for the hatred we share," Shawn stated.

"I'm the slime that'll make you famous, just remember that, Fraser," his boss informed him. "When this story prints, every newspaper across the country will want to run it!"

Shawn grabbed the tools he needed, ignoring his boss's excitement. "When I have something to report, I'll tell ye. Otherwise, I don't want to see yer face around here again," he warned before walking out of the shed, slamming the door shut behind him.

Brianna hummed the Ave Maria softly to herself while stringing rosary beads onto the thread, her weekly penance for her sins. She concentrated on the chore, trying not to think about the mound of beads still needing to be strung when the sound of splashing water distracted her.

Not wishing to be alone with her beads, Brianna gathered them all up and brought them into the kitchen to finish. Sister Mary Margaret would probably scold her for missing afternoon prayers and then take the sting off her reprimand with a sweet from her cupboards. She knew that the grandmotherly nun had to work hard at being stern with her soft heart.

When she stepped into the kitchen, her breath caught in her throat at the sight she viewed through the open door. It was that *same man* again, this time standing beside a washbasin, water glistening off his naked chest. He filled his hands with water, tipped back his head, and splashed the cool liquid down his body. Her eyes followed the tiny droplets as they slid down his slick skin, gliding over muscles that rippled the liquid downward. She struggled to gulp in air.

In the next instant, water splashed upon her face, startling her.

"Ye're no goin' to faint," the man demanded, tilting his face close to hers, his large hands gripping her shoulders while her body lay limp within his arms.

She opened her mouth to speak, but no sound came out.

"I should've never taken this job," he said, more to himself than to her. He meant only to apologize for startling her, maybe even gain her trust for his investigation, but her sweet rosebud lips were tempting him beyond control. He needed just one small taste of the forbidden fruit to satisfy his curiosity.

As if in harmony to his own thoughts, she lifted her mouth to his and *fainted* into his arms. Her handful of black beads fell out of her slack hand onto the floor, the sound of which jangled his nerves and brought him back to his senses.

Alarmed at how close he came to kissing a Catholic, he abruptly stood up. His action caused her to fall flat on her rump onto the floor. He grabbed his shirt and made his way quickly out of the room, but not before splashing the last of the water onto her face to bring her fully awake.

If he had to trip over this distracting nun every time he turned around, he'd never make any headway on his investigation.

CHAPTER TWO

The stench of Murdoch's Pub did nothing for his foul mood. Neither did the clutter of men, tired and irritable, crammed into the stagnant air of the tap house. He guzzled down his pint of whiskey, hoping to wash away the image of that irritating nun from his mind.

His eyes slowly glanced around the dimly lit pub, a habit he acquired over the years. He knew he tended to gather enemies rather than friends from the articles he wrote for various newspapers across the country.

When he was satisfied that he knew no one in the pub, he grabbed the bottle in front of him and left his seat at the bar to sit at an empty table in the darkest corner of the room, away from curious eyes.

The boisterous pub would not have been his first choice for a pint, but he shrugged his annoyance off, desperate for a drink. His frustration grew with every sip he took of the liquid. He didn't know what bothered him more – the distracting body of that red-haired nun that he couldn't seem to get out of his mind, no matter how hard he tried, or his vain attempts at finding any solid evidence of wrongdoings at the convent.

He heard the mutterings against the Pope and Catholicism in general as soon as he walked into the pub. The men were definitely ripe with suspicion and accusations towards the notorious convent on the hill. As soon as he sat down at the table, glasses raised high, including his own, to the cheer – Down with the Pope!

He didn't know if it was the bar's rowdy atmosphere or the whiskey that spurred his old anger to churn inside of him. He remembered his curiosity being tweaked when the first nun escaped the Charlestown convent two years ago with a string of stories of abuse within its walls.

When another nun ran off two weeks ago, only to be coerced back to the convent a few days later, he knew this story was for him. His years of waiting were over. Finally, he'd avenge his mother's death and disgrace the church his father chose over them.

As the evening progressed, tongues loosened, and Shawn listened very carefully to every angry word said. He knew the mere fact that these men worked long hours a day for a scrap of money didn't help their attitude towards anything, least of all the lush convent that towered over the brickyards, flaunting with every comfort imaginable to them.

"To hell with them all! 'Tis a prison on that hill filled with women for the priests to pleasure themselves," the barkeep stated.

"They're goin' to turn all those wealthy little Protestant gils enrolled in that demon school into nuns, they are," another man stated.

"Willin' or no!" a lad sitting at the bar behind him exclaimed, slamming his drink down onto the table.

"It jus ain't normal the way those women are forced to kiss the feet of them priests and lick the floor in the sign of a cross," a man wearing spectacles said before he took a swig of his pint, and the room grew quiet around him.

"Where'd ye hear such a thing, Sam?" the man beside him asked.

"That first nun that escaped been tellin' her whole story to some Boston paper," the man explained, adjusting his spectacles, clearly enjoying the limelight of privileged information. The ability to read singled him out in this illiterate crowd.

Sam stood and addressed the crowd. "Aye, I heard tell that nun that tried to run away last week is kept locked up in a cell inside that convent with no food or water. Her long red hair chopped to her skull in payment for her bad behavior. There's others that say she's already dead."

The man's voice rose with his anger when he stated, "'Tis not right, I tell ye!" He swiveled around when he spoke to the room of men at large. His red-rimmed eyes widened when they spotted Shawn.

"Hey, don't ye work at that convent? 'Ave ye seen the runaway nun?" the man asked, his Scottish accent heavy with the slur of liquor.

Shawn slowly shook his head. "No, I've never seen her." Then he hung his head over his drink, hoping to deter any more conversation from coming his way.

He came in here to distract himself from that nun only to have her brought back to the forefront of his mind. To find out that the one nun that tempted him every time he turned could possibly be the same discontented woman that ran away from the convent two weeks ago was ludicrous.

He sat back and mulled the idea over in his head. Nuns filled the convent. It was only natural that his mind swayed back to the *only* nun he met who happened to have red hair like the runaway nun. Not cropped short, but long and thick, fanning out in waves when he had placed her on her bed.

It irritated him that he couldn't control his own thoughts when she was around. He tried to bring her into his confidence, use her as a source on the story, but every time he was within inches of her, he lost all common sense. The need to run his fingers through the length of her thick, silky hair nearly overwhelmed him, as did the need to sup on those soft pink lips.

He shook away his carnal thoughts and drank deeply of the brew. Must be the idea that the woman was so damn unavailable that made her such a temptation.

Voices rose around him, breaking into his thoughts.

"We need to rescue them women from the clutches of the Catholic faith! And burn that devil's den to the ground!" someone cheered.

He heard the shout and sensed he had a limited amount of time to expose the convent before these men took matters into their own hands.

"Aye, to the ground!" came the cheer from the bleary-eyed men around him. The smell of whiskey filled the air as their glasses sloshed liquid onto the floor and each tin cup clanked against one another.

Shawn trudged his way up the convent's dirt drive with his head a bit clouded from the whiskey of the previous night. In the burgeoning light of dawn, his eyes drank in the grand brick façade of the elaborate three-story building before him. Ivy inched its way up the brick, covering most of the face of the building. Trees, heavy with fruit, lined the front entrance, and numerous stone paths twisted their way along lush gardens scattered all over the convent grounds. If he didn't know better, he'd think he stepped into the Garden of Eden.

Mallet swung over his shoulder, his eyes surveyed the length of fence which completely enclosed the convent grounds, searching for posts to reset when he spotted the notorious black-robed Superior at the top of the hill. Better to face the overlord of this den of heathens than avoid her.

"Mr. Fraser, just the man I wanted to see. I'm paying you to mend the fence and any maintenance work needed on the grounds, am I not?" the Superior stated into the silence of the early morning.

"Aye, ye are, Miss," Shawn replied, careful to keep his tone humble. "Is there a problem with me work, Miss?"

"None whatsoever as long as your work doesn't entail handling any of the women that live here, Mr. Fraser. You are not to speak or acknowledge any of my nuns, or you will be fired. Do you understand me?" she warned.

"Aye, I understand, Miss," he replied while he silently cursed the bewitching redhead for pointing him out to the Superior and nearly ruining his only way into the convent.

He watched the Superior walk back into the building, head held high, with only the light flapping of her long black garb disturbing the silence of the peaceful predawn.

The old knot of anger twisted inside him, ready to explode. He struggled to keep his fury under control, remembering that his exposé of the convent would be sweet payment enough to satisfy a debt long left unpaid.

He heard the first morning bell ring as he made his way inside the convent, turning down the hall towards the sleeping quarters. The woman had been a thorn in his side from the first time he stepped on convent grounds. He'd not be sent away because of her.

"Sleepin in again, are ye?" Shawn whispered into Sister Brianna's ear.

At the sound of his voice, her dream-filled eyes opened wide, and her sensuous mouth prepared to scream. In quick response, his lips covered her mouth before she had the chance to make a sound. He meant only to prevent her outcry but once he felt her soft lips pressed against his own, his inability to resist incited his anger.

He yanked her body hard against him. Sparks of desire raced through his bloodstream, fueling his blinding passion as his mouth moved over hers, demanding a response from her traitorous lips.

Conflicting emotions twisted and turned inside her. The savageness of his kiss confused her, though she felt safe and warm within his strong arms. An unfamiliar ball of heat began to form in the pit of her stomach, whirling her into oblivion where she could no longer think, only feel. Stars flashed before her eyes as she struggled to gain breath.

His fingers roamed freely over her face, combing through the thick mass of red hair hanging loosely onto her shoulders, his fingertips coming to rest on the creamy expanse of her neck. Blood pounded in his brain at each timid response to his touch, urging him without words to continue his onslaught.

His fingers moved to the top buttons of her cotton gown, desperate to feel the heat of her smooth skin below his fingertips when the sound of the second morning bell broke into his momentum. His movements skidded to a dead stop.

Stunned at his behavior, he stepped back and looked down at her lips, puffed and swollen from his assault. His eyes lowered to her cotton gown, half unbuttoned by his own lustful fingers, and his passion changed to fury.

"Now, ye listen to me. I've work to do here and don't need ye distractin' me from it. If need be, I'll go straight to your Superior and tell her everything!"

He threw his arms into the air when her eyes filled with tears. "This job isn't worth all this," he stated, and he walked out of the room. His lack of control over his own emotions sickened him.

Like father, like son, he thought with disgust. The sooner he finished this job, the better.

Father McBrien's warm smile of greeting did little to soothe her troubled mind. Brianna watched his slow gait into the parlor. His frame, once tall and overpowering, was now bent over with age. The few gray hairs he had left on his head, he kept smoothed back away from his face.

Since she was a young girl, she trusted this man with her innermost thoughts. It was only natural that she would call on him now when she had such disturbing thoughts. She bowed low before him.

"Rise, child. I can see by your face that much is troubling you. How can I be of help?" Father McBrien asked.

She nodded without words, not quite sure of where to begin. Hesitant to tell her trusted confessor the nature of the sin she committed. Although something familiar in the depths of his dark brown eyes urged her to confide in him.

"Whatever is said between us stays between us," he assured.

"Father McBrien, I really want to become a nun, but I'm not sure Mother will ever consent to it, especially if she knew what happened this morning," Brianna began. She stood and paced the floor of the room, her hands twisting at her waist.

Father McBrien lightly chuckled. "Nothing can compare to last week's escapade. The look of fear that crossed your Superior's face when she thought that something had happened to you is not something I can forget, nor should you. The Reverend Mother cares for you greatly and wants to make the right decision concerning your life. She's been your guardian for many years, trust in her advice.

I know growing up in the convent school you might have imagined a nun's life to be a bit romantic. But as you have seen for yourself, their day is made up of tedious chores along with their times of meditation with God. Now, tell me what happened this morning. I'm sure it's not as bad as you think."

Brianna took a deep breath before mumbling, "I kissed a man."

The old priest leaned forward in his chair and cupped his ear with his hand. "Speak up, child, my hearings not what it used to be. I thought you said you kissed a man," he chuckled.

"I did say I kissed a man," Brianna repeated, and she stepped back when the elderly man's body shot up off the chair.

"What!" Father McBrien stated.

Brianna's head hung down low. "If you're upset, Mother most definitely will be."

"Who is this man, and how did he get into the convent? Did you meet him in the gardens? Did he harm you?" Father McBrien stated, his face set in a frown.

When she didn't answer, he patted the chair beside him. "Sit down," he instructed in a much calmer voice, "Let's talk this through."

Brianna dropped to her knees in front of her most trusted advisor. "Please, forgive me, Father. A man kissed me, and I allowed it to happen, even enjoyed it, when my eyes should've been on the cross and only the cross." She tightly squeezed her eyes shut, her body full of remorse.

"God always forgives you, child," Father McBrien assured, lightly patting the top of her head.

"But will Mother forgive me? Have my actions ruined all chances of my ever obtaining the black veil?" Brianna grabbed hold of the elderly man's hands. "What will I do if Mother asks me to leave the convent?"

"Before you predict your Superior's actions, let's talk a minute about this kiss," Father McBrien said.

Brianna sat down beside him, wiping her tears with the back of her hand, making a conscious effort to calm down.

The elderly priest cleared his throat. "First of all, I'm glad you trusted me enough to tell me what happened to you. If you choose to live the life of a nun, there will always be temptations. This kiss was a perfect example. You need to think about what it means to you, or more importantly, what this man means to you."

"I hardly know him, but anytime I'm around him, I find it difficult to breathe," Brianna replied honestly.

"If gaining the veil is still most important to you, then you need to never see this man alone again," Father McBrien instructed, his face set. "Give me the man's name, and I will make certain of it."

"I don't know it," Brianna answered, her eyes wide.

"It will only help your cause if I speak to this young man and tell him of your intentions to become a nun. Tell me his name," Father McBrien urged.

"I really don't know his name, but I promise to never be alone with him again," Brianna assured.

"May the Lord help you follow the path that He has set out for you." His hand formed the sign of a cross in the air above her head.

It was just like Snead to *demand* to meet him here in the dead of night. He explained to him earlier today that he found nothing of a suspicious nature at the convent – yet. Except, of course, his involvement with the nun, which he would keep to himself. Rule number one – always stay detached from your subjects. If his involvement with the nun came out, his story would lose all credibility. He'd need to stay as far away as possible from her in order to keep some degree of sanity.

Snead actually had the audacity to ask him to write a fictional account of what he had seen working on the convent grounds. He increased the sum of money he was already willing to pay for this story and urged him to write the piece.

He admitted that, at times, his hatred for the church clouded his good judgement. And there was a second when he entertained the idea, but his integrity wouldn't allow him to lower to Snead's tactics and report facts that weren't true, no matter how great his distaste for the Catholic Church.

Snead, his cigar hanging out from the corner of his mouth, walked out of the darkness toward him, interrupting his thoughts. "There's a story to be found here, you just need to sniff it out," his boss said by way of greeting, his hoarse voice filled with determination.

"I'd like nothin' better than to expose these Catholics for what they really are. Something is happenin' inside that den of women besides prayin'. I'll discover it in due time."

He watched his boss mull over his words before speaking, shifting his cigar from side to side in thought. His eyes glanced uneasily into the darkness around them.

"Time is short. Try approaching this from the inside by charming one of those little women. I've heard tell you Scots got quite a talent for that."

"They're nuns, Snead! Brides of Christ! If ye think one of those women are goin' to welcome me with open arms, ye're crazy!" He hated the fact that the red-haired nun's innocent tearful face flashed before his eyes at that moment.

"Under the right circumstances, they will," Snead replied.

Before Shawn could question his boss's words, he looked up to see three men step out of the darkness behind him. One grabbed hold of his arms, the other two snickered in welcome as their fists slammed into his stomach.

"Don't overdo it, boys. He's one of my best writers!" Snead warned with a light chuckle before walking off.

The sound of Snead's voice incited his anger. He twisted loose and slammed his full body weight into his captor, smashing him against a tree trunk. The man slid to the ground unconscious. Shawn spun around as the other two men lunged toward him. One fist clipped his jaw. A lucky shot, Shawn thought, his mouth tasting blood. His fist smashed into the culprit's stomach in return, then picked him up and hurled him through the air.

From the corner of his eye, he saw the reflection of a knife as it sliced through the air, taking a chunk out of his arm before it pierced the skin of his leg. He moved quickly. His arm snaked out and twisted the arm of his assailant until he heard the crack of bone.

"I don't take kindly to anyone foolin' with me writin' arm," he gritted out, pushing his assailant's body away with the heel of his boot.

He searched the area for Snead while the three men scrambled away into the darkness. Damn, he should have guessed Snead was up to no good! The man was willing to do anything for a story. He'd make him pay for the little inconvenience he set up for him tonight.

His hands gripped the handle of the knife, set securely in his leg, and pulled the blade out. Then he pressed down hard on the gash to try to stop the flow of blood. His jaw ached like the devil, and the scrape on his arm was deeper than he first thought.

It looked like he'd have no choice but to ask for help at the convent. He'd never make it back to town, not with the amount of blood that drained from his leg.

At the side entrance of the building, he leaned heavily against the door, his legs weak. He rested the weight of his body against the wood, his heated cheek resting against its cool surface. Lost too much blood, his hazy senses told him. His fist pounded against the wood of the door, fighting to keep conscious. Dying on the steps of the nunnery would not do at all.

CHAPTER THREE

Brianna woke up startled. Her eyes flew to the candle that burned down low beside her. By the amount of wax that pooled around the candle's base, she knew hours had slipped by. Missing evening prayers, again, meant a stern lecture early tomorrow morning. She let out a weary sigh and swung her legs off her narrow bed and onto the wooden floor.

The sound of a loud thud against the back door caused her to quicken her step down the darkened halls of the convent towards the kitchen. When another knock sounded, she felt her first twinge of annoyance at the audacity of a visitor to call at such a late hour. Carefully, she tucked away the sinful feeling, knowing that she needed to work on her patience. Hadn't Mother just spoken to her about that last week and advised her to pray on it?

When she reached the door, she hesitated, took a deep breath, straightened her back and chin in a reserved manner becoming of a would-be Ursuline nun, and pulled open the door. The body came out of nowhere and fell heavily into her arms, causing her to crash backwards against the door that she had just opened. She cried out in pain, losing her balance and falling solidly onto the floor. The body followed her down, the weight of which slammed her head against the floor. She lay back stunned. When she came to her senses, she managed to scramble out from beneath his large frame to stand.

She poked her head out into the darkness. All was quiet outside with no sign of the culprits that did this harm to the man.

In order to close the door, she needed to push the man's limp body a few feet into the kitchen. She tugged the poor unconscious soul inside the door, then closed it firmly behind her. She stopped only to do the sign of the cross with a quick prayer that the man at her feet would not die before she returned, then rushed down the hall.

29

She returned with a hurricane lamp that she set on the floor beside his body. With shaky hands, she twisted his large frame over to face her, although she already had an inkling as to his identity. Turning him over confirmed it. His thick russet hair reflected red-gold streaks against the light of the lamp. Strands of hair fell in disarray over his slightly swollen, bruised face. The soft moans that escaped his lips told her that he was not dead – yet. And, for some odd reason her heart rejoiced.

His eyes fluttered open for just a second, and the pain that was written in the dark brown depths of them tore at her heart. She leaned over him, pushing back the strands of hair that had fallen over his bruised face, and gently tried to console him with softly spoken words, hushing him when he tried to speak.

"An angel are ye?" he rasped through swollen lips, his eyes rolling back in his head before he lost consciousness.

She flushed at his compliment, glancing down at the clothes she was wearing. The man must be delusional if he mistook her long white cotton nightdress and unruly length of hair spilling over her shoulder as in any way angelic.

His wounds would need tending and fast. Blood pooled beneath his leg. As much as she'd like to run to the chapel for help, she didn't want to leave him alone for any length of time. Her hands tore material off the hem of her dress and tied them tightly around the gash on his leg to try to slow the bleeding. Then she grabbed hold of his shoulders and as gently as she could, for fear of doing more damage, half dragged, pulled, and heaved his unconscious frame down the hall and to the room next to the kitchen.

Thankfully, it was empty, except for a small bed in the center of the floor. She hiked her dress up, totally unbecoming of a nun, she thought to herself, and climbed onto the bed, then leaned over and heaved his still form with all her strength onto the top of the bed. The man weighed a ton, everywhere she touched was hard-toned muscle. She jumped onto the other side of the bed and hefted him the rest of the way up onto the sheets.

Again, she hesitated. She could clearly see the extent of his injuries on his poor face and arm, but there was blood all over the rest of his body. Was it a sin to undress this man, especially such a supreme example of one, to look for more injuries? The only men she had ever seen over the past few years were Father McBrien and some fathers of the students that attended the school at the convent. Of course, these men were clothed at all times. And what of her promise to Father McBrien?

The man moaned softly in his sleep. She looked down at his still form and knew she needed to do whatever it took to help him, including undressing him to see the extent of his injuries.

Her hands shook slightly when she unfastened the buttons of his shirt. Taking deep calming breaths to slow her racing heart, she told herself that she needed to act like a proper nun in order to become one. Maybe helping this poor man would prove to Mother that she was deserving of the black veil of the Ursuline order, and her wait would be over.

A true nun would take care of an injured individual in a detached and practical manner, no matter if the injured were male or female. She voiced those thoughts repeatedly in her head as she washed away the blood from his chest to see additional bruises but no other scrapes. The blood looked to be from the gash on his arm and not from another deep wound.

She cleaned the deep wound on his leg as best she could, then refastened the bandage. She opted to wait for Sister Mary Louise if anything else needed bandaging below the man's waist. Some things were better put off until she had the courage of a full-fledged nun.

Once she felt she had done everything possible to make him feel comfortable, she closed her eyes to rest from the ordeal and wait until evening prayers were done. Then she could get some real help for the poor man.

At first, Brianna felt disoriented when the first soft rays of the early morning sun urged her lids to open and begin a new day. She stretched her sore back, wondering why she fell asleep on the hard chair instead of her soft bed. Her mind struggled to remember why she had done such a penance, until her eyes opened and stared directly at the heels of familiar leather boots resting on the bed beside her chair. The previous night's escapade came flooding back to her in a rush.

31

In the light of day, the size of the man, full of muscles and brawn, was made obvious. She couldn't imagine that she, herself, had hefted his enormous frame on top of the bed. His feet and legs extended a full foot over the length of the small bed frame. When her eyes traveled from his feet to his face, she was startled to see that he was wide-awake and staring straight at her.

She jumped out of her seat and felt the heat of a blush creep up her neck into her cheeks. She was ashamed to say that she boldly returned his gaze, mesmerized by the gold flecks that swirled in the dark brown depths of his eyes. Until her self-consciousness materialized itself again.

"Damn, not again," he said, his voice weak. "Deep breaths," he instructed, struggling with the pain it took to voice his demand.

She had been so fascinated by his eyes that she didn't realize that it was becoming difficult to breathe in the small room, the walls closing in on her. With her eyes still fixed on his, she took the deep breaths he demanded of her, slowly clearing her head and easing her breathing.

"Brianna, we've been looking all over for you!" her Superior reprimanded, then stopped, clearly stunned at the sight of the man in the bed at her side. As her eyes narrowed on the poor man, Brianna had a sudden urge to stand in front of him to protect him from her Superior's wrath.

"She's … an angel," the man voiced gruffly in her defense but Mother ignored him and turned to her, her displeasure apparent.

"Brianna, I will have a word with you outside," Mother demanded, her tone clipped, leaving no room for discussion. The flow of her long black robe sailing out of the room as quickly as it had appeared.

Brianna hurried out to do as she was bid, only glancing back briefly with an apologetic look at the man.

"What is that *man* doing there?" Reverend Mother nearly exploded in a harsh whisper. Brianna had never seen her Superior's eyes bulge quite so far from her face before. She sighed. She would definitely plead for extra time at confession next week.

"He was banging on the side door of the convent in dire need of help last night. Everyone was at prayers, and he was hurt and

32

bleeding and Ifellasleeponthechairbesidehim," she babbled on helplessly, her hands falling lightly to her sides.

"So you just took it upon yourself to drag him into the house in the middle of the night without saying so much as a word to anyone?" Mother exploded.

Brianna could see the amount of effort it took for her Superior to rein in her anger. Actually, she wouldn't be surprised if steam began to rise out of her ears.

Her Superior exhaled a deep breath and said in a much calmer voice, "Never mind, we will continue this conversation later today. What's done is done," she stated briskly, with one eye twitching slightly.

"I'm sorry, I didn't think," Brianna answered lamely.

Mother shook her head. "Do you not have chores to begin, Brianna?"

Brianna watched her turn around and walk sedately back into the room, her hands lost in the folds of her long black sleeves.

"Yes, Mother, I'll get right to them," she replied to her Superior's back.

Quickly, she made her way to the bedroom she shared with Sister Mary Louise, splashed cold water on her face, and donned a fresh white gown. Her hands flew to her face in shock. She had fallen asleep beside a total stranger, a man no less! She splashed more cold water on her heated face, then twisted the length of her disorderly hair into a tight braid before she dropped onto her bed.

Sister Mary Louise hurried into the room, interrupting her thoughts. She sighed deeply. Why couldn't she be more like Sister Mary Louise, with hair the color of spun gold, not one freckle marking her smooth skin, and eyes the palest blue she had ever seen? Besides her beauty, Sister Mary Louise always wore a cheerful smile on her face and a kind word ready on her lips.

"Thank the Lord you're all right, Brianna." At Brianna's dejected nod, Sister Mary Louise continued, "Is it true, then? There really is a man in the room beside the kitchen?" she whispered.

Again, Brianna nodded and watched Sister Mary Louise peek out the door of their bedroom. Brianna sighed with regret. Her eyes watered at the sight of Sister Mary Louise's black veil when she realized that she had ruined any chance of obtaining a black veil of her own.

"The Reverend Mother didn't look too happy when I asked her where you were this morning. Her eye kept twitching when she spoke. I lowered my eyes so that they wouldn't be drawn to the twitch." She covered her smile with her hand. "You're in a heap of trouble, aren't you, Brianna?"

"Unfortunately, Mother says that I act before I think. I'm certain that she will make me aware of that fact when she speaks with me this afternoon. Her anger prevented her from continuing her lecture on my bad decision making this morning," Brianna stated to Sister Mary Louise's wide eyes.

"Just do a super job on your chores, mind the rules today, and maybe with a lot of prayer the Reverend Mother will forget all about reprimanding you."

Brianna's shoulders slumped forward when she shook her head and looked over at Sister Mary Louise. She held back her tears so as not to upset her kind friend.

"I seriously doubt that. Not with the injured man lying in that bed to remind her each time she passes by his inert form. I just hope she doesn't decide to send me away."

The morning slipped quietly into the afternoon without word from the Reverend Mother, which only made her more anxious. Her impatience grew with each passing hour until she felt she couldn't take the suspense of her fate any longer. She strode into the Reverend Mother's office without knocking.

"Please, don't send me away! I promise to work harder at following rules and making better decisions."

Her Superior glanced up startled, then continued reading the paper on her desk, causing Brianna to babble on nervously to fill the silence of the room.

"Last night, I fell asleep and couldn't believe the time when I heard the bang on the back door. I know now that *maybe* I should have asked your permission before dragging a total stranger into the convent, but I made the immediate decision after seeing his battered body. Isn't a nun always charitable to all in need?"

Mother leaned forward on her desk, slapping her hands on the papers in front of her. "Maybe!?"

Brianna took a step back away from her desk, her eyes downcast. Now that she had her Superior's full attention, she wasn't quite sure she really wanted it.

"Didn't you think about the danger you could have been putting us all in by taking in that man in the middle of the night? There are people in town who would love to be rid of us. Of course, we pray that they will turn towards the one true religion and see the light, but until they do, we must try to be careful. It was a reckless decision you made last night, entirely without thought."

Brianna felt her eyes sting with tears threatening to fall as she stood despondently before her.

"I promise it won't ever happen again. Please, don't send me away." She knew of others before her that hadn't worked out as the Reverend Mother had wished. They were quickly escorted out to other convents that might be more suitable to them or sent back to town.

"Brianna, please calm down. I've been thinking lately that our community here might not be right for you." She put up her hand when Brianna opened her mouth to disagree. "I know I promised to let you give our life here a try instead of having you continue to board with the school girls, but I'm tending to think that you might be better suited to be a wife and mother. I've seen you working with the little ones at school. It might be a good idea to spend some time outside these walls before permanent decisions are made, ones that cannot be broken."

Brianna felt her face blanch at the word outside.

"Don't worry yourself, child," her Superior chided. "God doesn't want you to come to Him out of fear but out of joy."

"Yes, Mother, I'm going to try harder. I know this is what I was meant to do with my life. Please don't send me away," she pleaded.

Mother Superior nodded her head as Brianna turned and began to walk out of her office, her steps slow and measured with remorse.

"Oh, and Brianna," Mother's voice rang out and stopped her exit.

"Yes, Mother." Brianna slowly turned back toward the office, forcing a smile on her face.

"I'm assigning Mr. Fraser's care to you. You'll tend to his needs as well as your other chores you've been assigned."

"I beg your forgiveness, Mother, but I don't think that I can do that." When her Superior's eyes widened, she quickly added, "It's not that I don't want to do as you say, it's just that I have difficulty breathing around this man."

"Brianna, I didn't ask your opinion on this matter. Since you brought this man under our care, it only makes sense that you will take on the added burden to nurse him back to health."

"Yes, Mother," Brianna answered obediently.

She hurried down the hall, careful to keep her eyes downcast – *Rule Number Six,* she reminded herself on her way to Mr. Fraser's room. With her eyes focused on the floor in front of her, she ran straight into Sister Mary Margaret.

Startled, she quickly gripped the elderly nun's arms to prevent her from falling. "I'm so sorry," Brianna apologized with tears balancing on the edge of her lashes.

Sister Mary Margaret brushed her hands off and straightened her black robe. "No damage to these old bones. I do suggest you slow your pace and glimpse up from time to time when walking down the hall. You'll learn to understand the rules soon enough. Give it time, child," she encouraged.

Brianna twisted her hands in frustration. "I can't seem to do anything right!"

Sister Mary Margaret ushered her into the kitchen, her arm draped around her trembling shoulders. "Now, now, it takes time to get used to life here. I know you thought this was going to be easy. Pray that the Lord will help you to understand if you're meant to serve Him in this way."

"It was *so easy* being a student here," Brianna sobbed.

Sister Mary Margaret wiped Brianna's tears with a soft cloth. "It's good to have this trial period so you can question what is right for you. The Reverend Mother will help guide your way."

"I just know she's going to send me away," Brianna stated, wringing her hands together again.

"God has a way of directing our paths in life. Pray for guidance," Sister Mary Margaret urged, stilling Brianna's hands with her own.

"Don't worry so, listen to God's words of assurance."

Brianna wiped her eyes. "Thank you, Sister. I'm going to try harder, starting with the new task the Superior gave to me." She spun around with renewed determination, her thoughts already on what she would need to do.

When she peeked into her new charge's room, she was surprised to see him sitting on the edge of his bed, hunched over, struggling to remain upright. Brianna suspected, by the look of his pale face, that it took every morsel of his strength to sit erect.

She rushed to his side and tried to fluff the pillow behind him, which only added to his discomfort. "Please, don't overtire yourself, sir!"

"Damnation!" he rasped helplessly. What sort of horrendous crime did he commit that would place him back in the convent under the care of the one woman he wished never to see again?

Brianna did the sign of the cross right before his vision began to blur. Slowly, she eased him back down on the bed, which only irritated him further.

"Will ye please stop doin' the holy sign of the cross as if ye think I'm goin' to drop dead any moment!" he cried out in frustration.

"I'm not doing it for your sake," she snapped back, then covered her mouth in shame. A true nun remained patient with the sick and wounded and never lashed out at them.

She glanced over at his face, tight with pain, his lips set in a grim straight line, and felt appalled by her words.

"If there's anything you need – please ask," she stated with a forced smile.

"That won't be necessary. I can fend for myself," he growled back at her, slamming his arm against the bed, the quick movement loosening the bandage on his arm.

Quickly, she stepped forward to refasten the bandage. "I'm afraid everyone else was at evening prayers last night. I did the best I could do under the circumstances."

The words stuck in her throat when she stood so close to him, his eyes searching hers, the warmth of his skin below her fingertips. "If Sister Mary Louise was here, she would have done a much better job at it," she confessed, wringing her hands when she finished knotting the bandage.

"Aye, ye might be right," he replied, though she thought she saw a flash of a smile grace his lips.

The sound of his deep Scottish brogue slid over her body like a soft caress. She began to babble, feeling uncomfortable with the intimate feeling.

"Even Sister Mary Clarence, who teaches the children in the convent school, can bandage better than this. Sister Mary Margaret, on the other hand, can do just about anything, including a better bandage than that," she admitted, her face set in a frown.

"Yer name?" he asked reluctantly. It was too hard to ignore the worry in her voice. The girl had saved his life, which was no little task. If she didn't tend to him last night, he would have bled to death on the grounds of the convent. It bothered him being indebted to anyone, never wished to have ties like that. And the idea that he was indebted to a woman, a Catholic no less, made him miserable.

"Brianna Lawrence," she softly replied.

His eyes studied her in a way that caused her pulse to quicken.

"Miss Lawrence, please accept my apologies for my rudeness." He painfully stretched out his hand, which she accepted into hers. "Shawn Fraser. I thank ye for bandaging me last night. Without your help, I'm not sure how I'd have fared." He bit out the words, struggling to ignore the warmth that spread through his body by the light touch of her hand in his.

Brianna pulled her hand away, her mind racing back to the other morning, when she was awakened in a way that was more sinful than she was ever willing to confess to the Reverend Mother. She hid her hands behind her back. How would she live outside of the convent? Where would she go? Mother wouldn't send her away from the only home she knew, would she?

Mr. Fraser's lips moved in front of her, but she was unable to focus on his words over the roar in her ears.

"Breathe," he repeated, squeezing her arm until she began to acknowledge what he was saying with deep gulps of air.

When the late afternoon bell rung, she prepared to leave, then hesitated, remembering why she had come to his room. She said shyly, stuttering out, "I thought … like to read … while healing … brought … my book of prayers … need to go … bell ringing. You read latin, don't you?" she asked between deep breaths.

"Latin? Of course," he lied.

CHAPTER FOUR

Brianna hurried out of the room and down the hall, careful not to make too much noise lest she add to the sins she already accumulated during the week. She crossed over to the front door of the chapel and pulled the heavy wooden door open.

Today, she was late. Unfortunately, not a first for her. She heaved a deep sigh, disheartened by her actions but determined to do a better job today.

"Brianna, are you with us this morning? Your head seems to be in the clouds. As much as that does seem to be closer to heaven, I think God prefers for us to be on our knees in conversation with him," Mother Superior reprimanded.

Brianna blinked twice, realized she was standing in the open threshold of the door, and rushed over to a pew. Quickly, she knelt down, closed her eyes, and pressed her hands tightly together in prayer. She squinted open one eye to peek at Mother as she passed by her down the aisle. She'd need to try harder to wipe that look of utter resignation off her Superior's face if she were ever to become a member of this holy order.

Sister Mary Margaret's gnarled old fingers gently squeezed her shoulder, her eyes full of sympathy, as she followed behind the Reverend Mother down the aisle.

Brianna tried to concentrate on her morning prayers, but her mind kept wandering back to that man again. She'd never forget the way his deep brown eyes stared straight at her, causing her heart to race even now. She flexed her hands, remembering the feel of taunt muscle beneath his skin.

Shawn Fraser, she sighed, made her forget how to speak or even breathe. She found herself wanting to know everything about him. His long, slender fingers, with carefully manicured nails, led her to believe that he was not the typical hired hand that worked on the grounds.

Although he looked too rugged to be the sort of person that sat in an office all day, his long legs cramped beneath a desk.

The bells rang for the start of day. Brianna stood up, making a mental note to double up on her prayers at noon. She hoped that God would once again forgive her meandering mind.

Every time Shawn looked at Sister Brianna, he fought to keep hold of the hate he kept bottled up inside him toward all Catholics, including her. The thoughts filling his head were the sort that any decent man shouldn't be thinking about a young, innocent woman, especially a nun.

He felt he understood, firsthand, the talk that was going on around town. Women were made to be mothers and wives, not to live in a gated community, closed off from the world and against what God planned for them. It was unnatural.

He suspected that the Mother Superior had little choice of what to do with him. If she sent him back into town, one of her own hired hands, it would make her look ruthless and uncaring, increasing the tensions in town toward the convent. No, she'd give him time to heal, just like his boss had assumed.

Snead was desperate for this story, the large sum of money should have tipped him off. The cuts and bruises proved it. No, he wasn't about to thank his boss for his stay inside the notorious convent of Ursuline nuns. Nor would he ever forget the fact that Snead put him in a position where he was left to rely on Catholics for his care.

It was late that night when he finally had a chance to pull out the loose sheet of paper that had slipped out of Sister Brianna's prayer book. He moved the candle over to the edge of the table so that he could see the words written on the parchment more clearly.

He unfolded it, pushing aside the twinges of guilt he felt for invading her privacy. The parchment looked old and fragile. His eyes strained to make out the shape of faded angels splashed across the top, musical notes rather than words written below them. Why would she keep a faded song sheet in her prayer book?

"Mr. Fraser, would you like me to read your correspondence for you?" Brianna asked, walking into his room.

41

Quickly, he shoved the paper back into his pocket. "It's just Shawn, lass, but do you realize the time?"

"Yes, but I fear that my head is full of troubling thoughts, and sleep will not come easily to me tonight. I thought to check on you after evening prayers and make certain you didn't need for anything. Was that a personal letter?"

He ignored her question, his senses fully alert to a possible lead for his story, and asked one of his own. "What sort of troublin' thoughts could a nun possibly have in such a peaceful environment?"

"I'm afraid Mother Superior might send me away."

He tried with all his heart to ignore the strong urge he had to kiss the pout from her lips. "Send ye away for what?"

"My sins."

Shawn shook away his cloud of desire; his interest tweaked. "What sort of sin could ye have possibly committed inside a monastery?"

Her face became a bright red, mirroring the shade of her hair. "The kiss we shared, the fact that I bandaged you up without permission, I'm constantly late for prayers, and I can't seem to follow the rules here."

He struggled to sit up. "I thought ye were goin' to say ye killed a man. She'll send ye away for a kiss?"

"Maybe only a kiss to you, but for me it was a grievous sin. Once my Superior hears of it, my time here is over."

"Could she do that?" he asked.

"Yes, easily, but I'm going to try harder. My mind gets distracted sometimes, which makes me forget to do something or other. I break rule after rule, but I know I can do better, including staying away from temptation," she asserted, giving him a knowing look.

"Ah, I'm a temptation now." He couldn't stop the grin that spread across his face. "Let's test yer fortitude, lass." He rubbed his hands together. "Close the door."

"I will not," she stated firmly, her chin raised high.

"Close the door or I'll yell at the top of me lungs. Yer Superior will likely come runnin' and wonder why ye aren't takin' the best of care of me," he warned.

"That's not fair," she announced, hands on hips.

He opened his mouth to prove he was serious. She ran for the door – like he knew she would. He held in his chuckle and patted the space beside him.

"Now, have a seat beside me. I don't bite."

She sat primly on the chair, nose pointed upward with her hands politely resting on her lap. Her eyes stole several glances at the door.

"That tempted, are ye?" he asked, looking pointedly at the door, his eyebrow raised high. He cleared his throat. "What sort of punishment do ye get when ye break these rules?" He knew, firsthand, the domineering force of the Mother Superior.

"Any punishment that I receive is nothing compared to the disappointment I feel in my heart for failing to do my best," she automatically replied.

Damn, he felt guilty for getting the poor girl in trouble. Again, he reminded himself to stay detached, focus on the investigation of his story. He heard all the rumors about dungeons in the basements of this convent. It might take him a little time, but creating a bond with this girl might give him the information he needed. He pushed away the guilt he felt at deceiving her.

His fingers lifted a small tendril of her hair. "Yer hair 'tis lovely long and loose like that." He knew he said the wrong thing as soon as the words left his mouth and her cheeks spotted with circles of deep crimson. "Forgive me, I've embarrassed ye with my forward remark."

"I was readying for bed and didn't think to pin it up before coming to see if you needed anything. I'm sorry for disturbing you. If there's nothing you need, I'll take my leave," she replied, her eyes downcast, turning away in embarrassment.

He grabbed her hand to prevent her from leaving. "I've made ye feel uncomfortable with my remark, but I'm sure it's no the first time ye've heard remarks from men." For some reason, the thought of that alone made his hand clasp into a fist. Again, he reminded himself to stay detached.

"I've only heard the whispers of Sister Mary Anne and Sister Mary Margaret when they return from town. I've never ventured into town, never wished to go. My chores keep me busy enough right here."

"Never left these sacred walls, have ye? What age did ye first arrive here?" he asked, curious now. He didn't know if he was fishing out facts for the story or for himself.

"Eight years old. It was right after my mother died. I suppose my father didn't know what to do with me. He had his own grief and his business dealings and no time or energy left for me, so he brought me here to be schooled. It's been my home ever since. I'd better get back to my room."

"Let me set ye straight on one thing before ye leave. It was *I* that stormed into yer room that mornin' and took advantage of ye," he said with a nod.

"I allowed it to happen, even enjoyed it," she admitted with regret.

Enjoyed it, he thought, struggling to keep his smile hidden. Now, that was just the sort of honesty that would get her into trouble before long. Aloud, he said, "Ye had no choice." He moved closer to her to prove his point.

A thin space of air separated their lips. "No choice at all," he mumbled just as the candle flickered out beside the bed.

In the darkness of the room, a tear rolled off her cheek onto his lips, stopping him cold. He rested his forehead on hers. Words escaped him.

When she quickly pulled away to light the candle beside his bed, he couldn't help but notice the way her hand shook. Without a word, she hurried out of the room, the trail of long red hair disappearing from the candle's dim light.

An ache settled down deep inside his chest that had nothing to do with his bruises.

Brianna watched with envy as Sister Mary Louise began to dress, stopping only to kiss the finely pressed black habit and veil before putting them on. After donning the long black robe, she pinned her hair neatly under her black veil. The habit's only adornment, a holy cross, suspended on a surplice, hung from her waist. A gold wedding band, pledging her love to Christ, never left her roommate's finger.

Sister Mary Louise leaned over her bed and squeezed her hand. "Soon, Reverend Mother will see you deserving of the veil. Be patient, pray, and get up. You mustn't be late again for morning prayers," she urged with a sympathetic smile.

"I fear the more I covet the veil, the more it slips through my fingers."

"You try too hard, Brianna. Let God guide your way," Sister Mary Louise suggested.

Brianna swung her feet onto the cold floor. It was four in the morning and she longed to stay in bed one more hour, two would be ideal, three would be heaven, but she knew she had a matter of minutes to get dressed before walking down to the chapel for meditation.

She slipped pebbles into her shoes, *Rules of St. Ursula Number Eight, to remind her of her sins and help her to remember the rules of the convent.*

Slowly, she made her way to the chapel, careful not to make a noise at this early hour, *Rules of St. Ursula Number Five.*

When the Angelus bell rang, she knelt to begin her morning devotional prayers with a renewed fervor. Today, she would prove to Mother Superior that she was deserving of the veil and end her fears of being sent away.

She arrived early in the morning with a tray full of food for Mr. Fraser, hoping to impress the Reverend Mother with her diligent care of her charge. She needed to do everything possible to see that Mr. Fraser fully recovered. The sooner he recovered, the sooner he would leave the convent.

Before she reached his bedside, he spat, "Jus leave the tray."

She placed the tray on the table beside his bed and took two steps toward the door before turning around. Instead of leaving, she decided to sit beside him.

"What are ye doin'?!" he asked irritated, nearly tipping the tray onto the floor.

"I need to wait for you to finish so I can return the tray back to the kitchen," she stated simply, ignoring his angry disposition.

"I don't need any help," he warned.

"I didn't offer any," she replied.

"I can't eat with ye starin' at me," he added with a frown,

frustrated with the lust he felt every time she visited his room.

"Why are you always so angry?" Brianna asked in a calm voice.

His hands flew into the air and knocked over the tray of food she just brought him. "Angry, I'm not angry!" he shouted. "What do I have to be angry about!" he bellowed.

Brianna's knees sank to the floor. "Mother will be so upset with me. I must get you more food before she sees this mess," she mumbled to herself, hurrying to pick up every crumb of food that fell onto the floor.

Shawn heard her words and reached out to stop her frantic cleaning. "'Tis me own clumsiness that did this, not ye, lass."

"It's *my* job to take care of you, Mr. Fraser. I should have realized you were upset," Brianna stuttered, her eyes round with fear.

Shawn leaned over to where Brianna knelt and gently cupped her face in his hands. "Stop yer fussin'. 'Tis me own Scottish temper that caused this to happen." He was about to say something else, but the words slipped from his mind when he looked directly into the dark green depths of her eyes, pooling with liquid ready to fall.

His hands smoothed back the silky strands of hair from her face. The temptation to sink back into the velvety softness of her lips was too great an allurement. He needed to kiss away the hurt and fear that he caused her. Her sweet feminine scent intoxicating him, luring his lips closer to hers.

The Reverend Mother cleared her throat behind them.

Brianna jumped back alarmed and fell flat on the floor. Her face drained of all color before it became a bright red when she looked up at her Superior.

"I see that you're in good hands, Mr. Fraser. I'm sure that Brianna will make certain that your recovery period is a short one," Reverend Mother stated with a smile before she turned and walked back out of the room.

Brianna sat back, stunned at the grin that flashed across her Superior's face, making her hope soar that soon she would be invited to be a full-fledged nun and able to stay in the convent forever.

Mr. Fraser's attitude didn't improve much after he ate his bread and tea. Actually, it seemed to get worse by the end of day. With this in mind, she arrived promptly at his side with a tray full of food for his evening meal, careful not to be late and irritate him further.

"Jus leave the tray," he muttered.

Brianna sighed, did her Superior realize how difficult this task was before she assigned it to her?

"Leave it, I'll feed myself!" he barked at her when she stood motionless.

Brianna said a silent prayer for patience before setting down his tray beside him.

Reverend Mother strode inside the room. "Is everything all right in here? I heard yelling," Mother stated, her eyes looking curiously at the two of them.

"Of course," Brianna answered. Her frightened eyes glancing quickly over to Mr. Fraser.

"Do you agree, Mr. Fraser?" Mother asked while Brianna held her breath.

"Aye, things are fine," he assured. "Jus a bit irritable bein' stuck within these four walls. I'm used to workin' outdoors, breathin' in the fresh air, not lyin' in a bed nursin' me wounds all day."

"Brianna, why don't you bring Mr. Fraser outside? The fresh air might speed up his recovery. That is what you want – to speed up your recovery, isn't it?" Mother asked Shawn.

"Of course," Shawn replied, his conscience feeling the sting of guilt.

Brianna shook her head. "I've much praying to do. I should have seen your need before my Superior suggested it," she whispered more to herself than to him.

No, he said to himself. If she knew the *need* he had for her, she would run out of this room and never return. He was certain of that.

CHAPTER FIVE

Shivers of delight danced down her spine, warming her more than the hot afternoon sun. She tried to concentrate on the words he spoke, but it was impossible when his breath blew softly against her ear.

"Are ye confined here, Miss Lawrence? Treated bad? Ye can confide in me," Shawn whispered as they both sat on the wooden bench in the gardens.

Until the meaning of the words hit her.

She abruptly stood up, hands on hips, nostrils flaring. "This is my *home*, Mr. Fraser. I loved being schooled here by the Sisters. When I finished my courses at the academy, Mother was kind enough to let me stay on to become a nun. I don't ever wish to leave."

He knew he had only a limited amount of time left in the convent. Here, away from listening ears, he tried to gain her confidence. "I've upset ye," Shawn began, and he placed his hand on her arm to prevent her from leaving.

"Aye, I did indeed," he continued. "And I'm to beg yer forgiveness for that. Especially since I've a favor to return for all the help ye've done for me, and for all the trials I've put ye through," he said with a nod, his chin set stubbornly.

It was her turn to look chagrined, ashamed of her easy temper. "I did what I did out of kindness and expect no return for it."

"All the more reason for me to repay your kindness."

She sat back down on the bench beside him and breathed in the sweet fragrance of flowers growing in the gardens around them. It calmed her sitting amid the lush foliage with the ivy climbing and twisting its way over the back of the bench. Deep pink peonies flopped their heavy blooms over short stalks of purple irises. Clumps of cheerful yellow daylilies bordered stone paths. Lavender and white phlox crept their way along stones and crevices winding colorful paths throughout the gardens.

"'Tis beautiful here." He stretched his long legs out in front of him and leaned his face up to the sky.

It was good to hear him state what she had always known. This place created beauty inside and out, from the tranquility of the lush gardens to the inner sanctity of the blessed chapel. She knew she would do anything to stay here forever.

Shawn grabbed hold of her arm with a little squeeze to interrupt her thoughts. "I'm a good listener."

"Oh, I'm so sorry, Mr. Fraser, my mind wanders easily. Let me show you the vineyard. The bishop himself helped to plant the grapevines. The orchards are brimming with apples ready to be picked, and the gardens are overflowing with vegetables and herbs. There's a flower garden over that way. Let me show you." She hurried along the path, anxious to change the subject of their conversation.

"I only made the comment to let ye know if ye ever need me, don't hesitate to ask." His voice grew hoarse with exertion as he tried to keep pace alongside her.

With the flower garden in sight, she rushed toward the blooms. "Look at these lovely blossoms," she said a bit too enthusiastically, ignoring his comment. Struggling not to let anger make her say things she would later regret.

When she turned toward him, she noticed the way his face grimaced in pain with each step he took. Ashamed at ignoring his needs as well as his words, she led him to the nearest bench.

It worried her that she walked too far down the path on his first day outside. "Would you care to go back inside?"

"No, I'm fine," he stated, wearing a crooked grin. He slowly lowered his body onto the bench.

She knew that he wasn't fine, but when those warm brown eyes looked up at her, she lost all thought. The fact that her hand ached to rub against his freshly shaven face confused her. She took two steadying breaths.

The sound of children laughing interrupted her wayward thoughts. "Brianna!" a group of little girls shouted, waving and running up to her. "We miss you," they chattered, surrounding the bench.

"Will you read us a story? Sister Mary Clarence doesn't change her voice for the different characters like you do," Jessy stated innocently. Her curious eyes studied Mr. Fraser. "Who are you?"

Brianna quickly answered. "Girls, this is Mr. Fraser. He's here for a short visit while he recuperates."

Little Samantha pointed at his bandages. "What happened to him?"

Shawn changed his voice to sound like a sailor, low and throaty. "Wounds came from defending treasure my shipmates and I discovered on a deserted island off the coast. Band of pirates attacked our ship and tried to steal the treasure we found, but we held our own, except for a few small scratches." He held up his arm for all to see.

"Really?" Jessy asked. The girls gathered closer for a better look at his bandage.

Brianna narrowed her eyes at him until he let out a long breath and confessed the truth. "No, nothing that excitin' I'm afraid, little one. Stumbled over me own two feet."

Brianna gave him a wide smile for his honesty.

"Jus havin' a little fun," he added, rubbing the top of Jessy' head.

Sister Mary Clarence clapped her hands. "That's enough, girls. Let's not tire Mr. Fraser." She turned to him. "Good to see you up and about. I can see that Brianna is taking good care of you. You've a healthy imagination, sir."

Shawn gave a slight nod before he moved to get up, leaning heavily on the crutch she fashioned for him. Automatically, Brianna hurried to his side, placing her arm around him for additional support.

"I'm afraid I tired you with our walk. Lean on me," she offered.

Without thought, Shawn leaned against her soft shapely form, enjoying the silky feel of her skin against his own. Until he came to his senses and stepped back in alarm, causing him to lose his balance and fall smack onto the dirt of the flowerbed. A tall yellow sunflower tipped over to rest on top of his head.

"Damn!" he muttered under his breath, brushing the flower aside with his hand. He forced a smile on his face for the sake of the ten little girls pointing and giggling at his ridiculous body lying on top of the flowerbed. Inside, he cursed his boss for putting him in this situation. All this pain and frustration for nothing. There was no story to be had here, the bruises he took for no reason at all. On top of that, he was lusting every second of the day after a nun.

Frustrated, he pushed himself up, waving off her help, and held onto the nearby bench for support. "'Tis in no way yer fault. I'm no the best company."

"Are you all right? Maybe I should get help," she stated, wringing her hands frantically in front of him, which only made him feel worse for his outburst.

"No, I'm clumsy, but fine. Is there a cellar to this place?" he inquired, trying desperately to keep his mind focused on his work.

When she looked up at his blunt attempt at investigative work, he added, "I did a bit of building work a few years ago. I'd like to see the beams that hold up such a grand structure." It was a lame explanation, but she believed him.

She frowned at the way he stood unsteadily before her. "Are you sure you'll be able to maneuver down the stairs in your condition?"

"No, not sure, but I'll try. Have ye ever been down there?" he continued.

"No, never had a reason to go down. I've only seen Sister Mary Margaret store root vegetables down there in winter."

"Have ye seen the Reverend Mother venture down there?" he asked. When she looked at him strangely, he added, "I've to wonder as to how safe 'tis down there."

He hobbled behind Sister Brianna to the door of the basement. It was nearly hidden in the dense ivy that climbed up the brick on that side of the building. A padlock hung from the knob of the door. Before he had the chance to ask the location of the key, she dropped to her knees with her face lowered to the ground.

Shawn glanced around behind him. An elderly priest stood quietly watching him. His eyes flickered back to Brianna's inert form bowed low before him. He clenched the fist that wanted to slam into the gut of the egotistical man of God. The arrogance of these men sickened him.

"You may rise, child," the priest instructed. The man extended his hand to Shawn. "I'm Father McBrien, good to see you feeling better, lad. Has the hospitality been adequate?"

Shawn swallowed down the bile that rose in the back of his throat, ignoring the hand offered. He had known this day would come, but nothing prepared him for the force of emotions that raced through his body coming face to face with his father for the first time.

Sister Brianna looked at him oddly. He tried to force a smile on his face for her sake, knew she'd only worry and blame herself, if, in fact, his hand slammed into this old man's stomach. Even though the man deserved to be knocked off his self-righteous pedestal.

He restrained his anger and stated through gritted teeth, "Aye, more than adequate."

"Brianna, Sister Mary Margaret is looking for you," the priest announced, dismissing her. Shawn watched her bow her head and hurry off. Again, he swallowed his anger, watching Sister Brianna do as she was bid.

"You don't like me, do you?" the old priest stated, amused.

"Your observation is fairly adequate. Though the word despise comes to mind whenever I think of my *father*." He watched the color drain from his face, then waited a heartbeat before he stated, "Does the name Abigail Fraser mean anything to you, Father McBrien?"

The old man leaned an unsteady hand against the brick wall of the convent. "The name doesn't sound familiar. Should it?"

"My mother wrote several letters to her aunts describing her relationship with you. Your name is clearly stated in those letters, if you have thoughts of denial."

"I hate to disappoint you, but I've never met your mother. I'm a priest, lad, taken sacred vows to remain celibate my entire life. This must be some sort of mistake."

"Tell that to the grave of my mother," Shawn spat at him.

A coughing fit assailed the old man, but Shawn made no move to help him. A nun quickly rushed over with a cup of water. His father's face turned several shades of purple before he was able to open his mouth to speak. "I don't know what's come over me. Maybe the heat," he muttered.

"Should I help you inside, Father McBrien?" the nun asked.

"No, thank you, I'm fine now. Go along," he assured her.

"Ye expect me to believe ye? Ye took advantage of my mother with sugarcoated words, then rejected her when she became pregnant with me. Made her feel so vile that only days after I was born, she took her own life. Don't give me your lies!" he exclaimed in a hushed whisper.

The priest shook his head, walked to a nearby bench and sat down. He rubbed his hand down his face. "I never knew."

"Ye never cared to know what happened to her as long as she was far away from here," Shawn stated.

"I cared deeply for your mother, but when she told me she was with child, my child, I felt the ground fall away from my feet. I was young, priesthood just given to me days before her announcement. I couldn't turn my back on God. I couldn't give all that up, not even for you."

"Much easier to get rid of my mother," Shawn spat.

"No, I lived with the pain of my decision every day of my life. Years later, I was tempted to come look for you but knew it wouldn't be the right thing to do. We had gone our separate paths, and my showing up at her doorstep would only cause pain."

"I don't wish to hear your lies. Ye'll pay for what ye did to my mother."

His father shook his head sadly. He stood up, then turned back toward Shawn. "Nothing I do or say will take away your pain. I just ask that you remember the kind hospitality you received here when you venture back into town. Revenge is a powerful two-edged sword," the priest added.

Shawn shook off his words with disgust. "'Tis too late for ye to ask anything of me. I'll leave this place first thing in the morning."

Brianna's foot tapped nervously on the wooden floor, waiting for her Superior. She knew it was never a good sign to be summoned to her office.

Mother swept into the room in a swirl of black. She took a seat behind her desk, swept off her spectacles, and smiled, which only heightened her anxiety.

"I promise to do better, Mother. I've been praying day and night. I haven't broken one rule today. Yes, I know it's still early morning, but I've a feeling that today will be perfect," Brianna stated, forcing her voice to sound cheerful.

"I agree, because today I've decided that you will accompany Sister Mary Margaret into town to help with her errands. Since you no longer need to care for Mr. Fraser, you will have ample time to help her out today."

"I can't do that, Mother."

"I didn't ask your opinion on the matter, Brianna," Mother asserted.

"Mr. Fraser left? Without saying good-bye?"

"Early this morning. He thanked us for our hospitality," Mother replied.

Brianna sat back in her chair, confused. Why did she feel this twinge of disappointment? She should be happy that her chores had been lightened. Instead, she felt like a tiny hole had been pierced through her heart.

Mother snapped her fingers in front of her face, bringing her back to the problem at hand. "Brianna."

"I'm sure Sister Mary Louise would be pleased to go into town in my place. She'd be much more helpful than I could ever be. I know I'd be an added nuisance to Sister Mary Margaret," Brianna explained.

"As I said earlier, you need to experience life outside these convent walls before making a permanent vow to God. Let Him guide your ways, Brianna. You may be surprised at where He leads you."

"Yes, Mother," she answered, her eyes downcast.

"Please erase the glumness from your face before you accompany Sister Mary Margaret. Her feelings are fragile, and you wouldn't want her thinking that you didn't wish to go with her today, would you?" Mother asked, her voice clipped and sharp.

"Of course not, Mother," Brianna replied.

Shawn paced the floor of his bedroom deep in thought. He'd stop, glance at the slip of paper he'd found posted in town, then start pacing again. This morning, when he arrived back at Mrs. Benson's boarding house, he'd reread the warning that was nailed to every building, fence, and rail in town.

The posters were addressed to the selectmen, warning that the nunnery in Charlestown would be destroyed by the truckmen during the month of August, if an investigation were not made at the convent concerning the runaway nun.

He'd heard rumors that a group of men had formed to plot against the convent, dissatisfied with the brief investigation the selectmen made into the matter. Of course, angry talk was one thing, but taking the law into your own hands was another.

Was he willing to risk the possibility of Sister Brianna being harmed at the convent if these men followed through with the threats they made?

When he left Mount Benedict this morning, he promised himself he'd never return. Without a full exposé to shove into his sacrilegious father's face to avenge his mother's good name, he had no interest to stay in this town. He'd get his revenge elsewhere.

Brianna gripped the side of the wagon, her fingers digging into the wood sideboard as the horses carried them into town. She prayed continuously, hoping this nightmare trip would all be a dream. She didn't want to experience life outside of the convent. *Lord, please send me back home.*

"There's no use making a fuss about this," Sister Mary Margaret announced.

Brianna glanced up at the elderly nun beside her. The wind lifted her thick silver hair tucked neatly beneath her black veil. She held the reins of the horses and steered the carriage skillfully for a woman of her late age.

"Fuss?" Brianna asked.

She patted Brianna's knee with her wrinkled hand. "Don't help worrying yourself to a frenzy. Better to face your fears – head on. The Lord will be by your side, so stop fretting."

"I'm happy at the convent. I don't need any new experiences," Brianna said, her voice rising in agitation.

"Relax, Brianna, and let God guide you instead of your fears."

"Easier said than done," Brianna confessed.

She tried not to look at the sights before her as the carriage approached town, but against her will, her eyes peeked open, and to her utter amazement, excitement instead of fear began to bubble up inside her.

Carriages, wagons, horses, and riders filled the main road in town. Boardwalks crowded with mothers tugging small children behind them, city men in suits, and field hands in overalls. Her eyes darted into all directions in order to see everything, the post office at the center of town, general store on her left, barber on her right with a millinery shop beside it.

Before she knew it, Sister Mary Margaret stepped down from the wagon and looped the reins of the horses over the hitching post. Brianna followed close behind her.

"I've supplies to get from the general store. Would you please walk over to the post office and check for any post for the convent?" Sister Mary Margaret requested before walking off toward the general store.

Brianna hurried up next to her. "Alone?"

"Brianna, the post office is only a few feet away from the general store. Go now, and meet me back at the general store." She shooed her along with her hand.

Brianna stood frozen on the wooden boardwalk. She closed her eyes against the dust that flew up from the wheels of carriages traveling by her. When she began to get in the way of people walking down the boardwalk, she forced her feet to move in the direction of the post office. Once inside the building, she gathered the convent's mail and made her way back over to the general store, feeling proud of herself.

When a young girl, Jessy's size, looked up at her strangely, she smiled in return. The mother grabbed the child's hand and pulled her away.

"Is that a nun, mama?" the girl asked, her eyes wide with fear.

"Hush, child, we don't talk to no Catholics!" the mother reprimanded.

Before Brianna could cross the boardwalk and enter the general store, an older boy stopped and rudely pointed his finger into her face. "Look, it's the runaway nun!" When his friends stood silent, he added, "It has to be her, look at her dress and the color of that hair!

I told you they wouldn't kill her!"

The boy's words made people stop and stare. It was difficult for her to take a breath with so many people crowding around her, their closeness suffocating her. They pointed and stared, shouting cruel words about the Reverend Mother. When she couldn't stand to listen anymore, she covered her ears with her hands and tried to shove her way through the crowd, but the people formed a tight wall around her.

Shawn had just entered the newspaper office across the road to chew out Snead for his perverse business tactics when he noticed the crowd on the sidewalk. His reporter instincts kicked in as he limped his way steadily across the street to investigate. When a flash of red caught his eye, his mind raced back to the contents of the poster he had just read, and his hobble turned into a run. He didn't know what the people of this town were capable of doing anymore.

His alarm increased when he spotted Brianna standing in the center of the crowd, her face wet with tears, and a look of stark terror on her face. When her eyes began to roll back in her head, Shawn forcefully shouldered his way through the crowd and scooped her slim body into his arms before she hit the ground.

Automatically, his eyes scanned the crowds for Sister Mary Margaret, who normally made the runs into town for supplies. He spotted the elderly nun stepping out of the general store, her face confused. Her eyes widened when she saw Brianna in his arms.

She elbowed her way next to him. "What's happened?"

"No time to explain. Where's yer wagon, Sister?" Shawn asked.

"Follow me. I came out as soon as I noticed the group of people gathering around Brianna. Why would they do that?" Sister Mary Margaret asked, her breathing heavy as she hurried toward the wagon.

Shawn ignored her question and jumped onto the bench of the wagon with Brianna in his arms. He wouldn't relax until he had Brianna safely back inside the convent.

"Can ye drive this rig, Sister?" Shawn asked.

"Can I?" Sister Mary Margaret answered, with a slap of the reins against the horses' backs. "Can birds fly?" she asked with a wink of her eye.

The horses lunged forward and Shawn's arms tightened on Brianna's body. "Steady pace, Sister. We don't wish to arouse more attention than we already have."

Shawn was so intent on escorting the two women safely back to the convent that he didn't notice Brianna had opened her eyes until he heard her voice.

"Why do they hate me?"

"'Tis the religion, not ye, lass," Shawn answered, his eyes glancing behind the wagon, making certain they weren't being followed. He worried that the men in town might think to rescue Sister Brianna from the convent and frighten her even further.

"They called me the runaway nun as if they knew me," she stated confused.

She blinked back tears, just realizing that she was lying in the arms of Mr. Fraser. Quickly, she sat up and squeezed onto the bench beside Sister Mary Margaret, straightening the folds of her dress. "You never said good-bye."

"I was in a bit of a rush to leave." His eyes met hers. "I'm sorry, lass."

"How did you know I needed help?"

"I glimpsed the red of yer hair from across the street and knew by the look of yer pale face that ye were in trouble."

Brianna turned to Sister Mary Margaret. "I fainted – again."

Sister Mary Margaret gave her a sideways glance. "Again, Brianna?"

"She's made a habit of faintin' in my presence," Shawn explained before Brianna had a chance to answer.

Sister Mary Margaret gave him an odd look before her body slumped forward. She would have fallen under the wheels of the buckboard if not for his quick reflexes. With one hand holding on to Sister Mary Margaret's limp form, he tried to grab hold of the reins before they slipped off the wagon onto the horse's backs.

"Oh, my Lord! Sister Mary Margaret! What's happened to her?" Brianna exclaimed.

Shawn shifted the elderly nun's body toward Brianna. He balanced his body on the edge of the wagon, leaning over as far as he could to reach the leather straps.

"Be careful you don't fall!" Brianna shouted over the noise of the galloping hooves of the horses.

He glanced back at her, one dark brow arched high. "I'll try not to do that."

His fingers stretched as far as they could toward the dangling reins. Without any notice, the horses turned the corner of the dirt road toward the convent. Shawn grabbed hold of the straps and maneuvered his way back onto the bench of the wagon.

He pulled back on the reins to slow the horses to a more manageable pace. "Whoa."

Once he felt he had the horses under control, he turned to Sister Brianna. "She must have fainted. Convent women seem to make a habit of that. No need to worry, we'll have her back at the convent soon enough."

Brianna rocked Sister Mary Margaret's body in her arms with tears streaming down her cheeks. "How could I have done this to her?"

"What are ye talkin' 'bout? Ye had nothin' to do with this. Loosen the cowel around her neck. She looks warm," he stated.

Brianna squeezed her eyes shut. "It was all my fault. If I didn't come today, Sister Mary Margaret wouldn't have become so overly excited over the mishap, and you wouldn't have had to risk your life to gain control of the horses."

Shawn steered the wagon through the gate of the convent and up the drive. "This isn't your fault. Could be the oppressive heat racking her aged body. Do you understand me?" He sent her a sideways glance to emphasize his point.

"I don't know what I would do if anything happened to her."

His wrists flicked the reins of the horses. There were no words of assurance to give her. The very young and very old were always susceptible to the diseases that ran rapid through the towns.

It seemed that every person in the convent had a special place in Sister Brianna's heart. She never spoke an unkind word about anyone, rather she treated them all like family.

Why would the people in town think her to be the runaway nun? Her fear of being asked to leave dispelled all those theories as nonsense. If not for the red of her hair, there would be no question in his mind.

The sight of the Reverend Mother rushing out to the wagon interrupted his thoughts. He'd never seen her move that quickly.

"What happened?" she asked, worried, her usual reserved manner absent.

He carried Sister Mary Margaret's limp body into the convent. "She fainted on the wagon, her body feels hot to the touch."

"Lay her down on the bed. We'll take over from here, Mr. Fraser."

During the days and nights to follow, Brianna took her turn praying by Sister Mary Margaret's bedside. The Reverend Mother insisted that at least one nun prayed over her body at all times.

She bit down hard on her lip, holding back tears. Sister Mary Margaret hardly looked like herself, her face gaunt and her body emaciated from the silent disease that wracked her body.

Stifling hot air filled the darkened room. She knelt beside the bed, careful not to disturb Sister Mary Margaret's rest. With rosary beads in hand, she fervently pleaded with God to save Sister Mary Margaret.

She glanced to her side, where the Reverend Mother knelt, her hands busy with beads. "Mother, is there still hope?"

The Reverend Mother slowly lifted her weary eyes. "There is always hope with God."

"But she takes no food, not even sips of broth," Brianna whispered.

"We mustn't give up hope. The Lord will answer our prayers. He would not turn his back on us in our time of need," the Reverend Mother announced with conviction.

It worried Brianna that the Reverend Mother never left Sister Mary Margaret's side throughout the ordeal, not even to eat. Sister Mary Clarence explained that the two nuns had been together for many years and had formed a special bond.

The vigil continued for several long days.

Brianna stood outside of Sister Mary Margaret's room and waited with the other nuns for the doctor's report. It came several minutes later when the door opened. The Reverend Mother followed the doctor out of the room and announced that dear Sister Mary Margaret had succumbed to the dreadful disease of tuberculosis.

A fog of grief blanketed the halls of the convent.

Brianna escorted the doctor to the front door on shaky legs, her heart numb. She didn't think she would ever forget the stiff gray composure of the Reverend Mother when she delivered the dreadful news.

This only made her worry more when she searched every room and throughout the grounds for her Superior, to find out that she seemed to have disappeared. Hours passed. When she was about ready to give up her search, a slight movement behind the barn caught her eye.

"Mother, is that you?" she stated, approaching the far back corner of the barn.

She rounded the corner and stopped dead in her tracks. On the ground in a flood of black lay her beloved Superior. An empty wine bottle sat at her side.

Brianna rushed over and lifted the Reverend Mother's veiled head onto her lap. "Wake up! You can't die, there has been enough death for today."

To her surprise, her Superior's eyes fluttered open. "Brianna, stop fussing and help me up."

Her arms hefted her Superior's body and rested her shoulder against the wood of the barn. She brushed the grass and leaves scattered across her dress.

"Should I go for help? Are you ill, Mother?" Brianna asked, her voice filled with worry.

The Reverend Mother blinked several times, her eyes squinting to focus. Her hands held on to the wood of the barn while her body wobbled as if the earth moved below her feet. She shook her head and lifted her chin with authority, which did much to calm Brianna.

"No need for help. I shall rely on you, Brianna, to get me safely back to my room to rest, and you shall not repeat what you have seen here to anyone. Do you understand me?"

"Are you going to die like Sister Mary Margaret?"

The Reverend Mother's face softened. "No, I am not."

61

CHAPTER SIX

The poster gnawed away at his conscience, leaving him with an uneasy feeling that he couldn't seem to shake off no matter how hard he tried to ignore it. Warning the Mother Superior of possible danger would clear his conscience. Then he'd make certain Sister Brianna was out of danger.

Shawn balanced from one foot and to the other, shaking his head at the fact that he was standing at the front door of the convent so soon after he left, especially since his intention was to never return.

He knocked on the wooden door. The Reverend Mother, herself, opened the door. It startled him to see the physical change in her face that came about with the death of one of her nuns.

"Mr. Fraser, back so soon?" Mother Superior asked, one eyebrow lifted high, her tone deceptively soft.

"'Tis a serious matter I've come to discuss with ye," he announced, pacing the floor in the front parlor, not sure of how to begin.

"Please, sit down. Whatever the problem, I'm sure we can resolve it," she assured him.

"I'm no too certain of that," he said, shaking his head. "I also would like to pay my respects. Sister Mary Margaret was a good person."

"Thank you," the Reverend Mother replied with a nod.

He twisted his hat in his hands and thought about how to approach the subject.

The Reverend Mother cleared her throat loudly, bringing him back to the present and why he was here today.

"I've reason to believe that there are groups in town planning to burn down the convent," he stated.

Before she could comment, he added, "My sources are reliable men. There is a definite threat here to the building and the nuns."

She shook her head and brushed aside his information with a

wave of her hand. "The threat has always been there, Mr. Fraser. My question is with you, sir. I knew from the moment that I hired you that you worked at the newspaper office. I gave you every opportunity to inspect our grounds without restriction. Why is it that you have been sent back to me with this information? Is this an additional little story you want to add to the one you're already writing on us?"

The Superior's question was forthright, he had to hand it to her as well as any other man that threw the truth of the situation into his face. Many men squirmed under his direct gaze, instead it was he who felt the need to squirm. He decided that a straightforward question deserved the same in return.

"Aye, 'tis true when I first arrived here, I was sniffing out the idea of a story but it seems the beating I took was all for naught. I found no suspicious tale enclosed in these cloistered walls. *This* threat is real though. If you choose to ignore it, then I'd like to at least take Sister Brianna out of here for an extended vacation with my aunts in Halifax, Nova Scotia, just until the danger passes. I don't want Sister Brianna's life in danger."

"I'm afraid you're under a misconception, Mr. Fraser. Brianna is not a nun. As much as she wishes to become one of us, I'm not at all convinced that she would be right for this sort of, well, for lack of a better word, tranquil life." She stopped and looked straight into his eyes when she continued, "She may be better suited to life as a wife and mother. I can imagine her becoming a wonderful mother after seeing her with the young students here."

He was feeling a bit uncomfortable with the direction of the conversation. His head still spun over the simple fact that Brianna wasn't a nun and why she had never felt it necessary to clarify that point with him.

The Mother Superior's eyebrow rose over his suddenly pale face. She added briskly, getting up to conclude their conversation, "As I stated before, the threat has always been there, it is nothing new. Brianna is perfectly safe within these walls. We only pray that the hearts of these men will change."

"I mean to do more than pray, beggin' yer pardon. I need to get Brianna out of here. I owe her that much for all the kindness she has shown me."

He watched her slip her hands into the folds of her black robe, preparing to leave the room. "Your gratitude is noble, but she's too young to venture on such a long trip unescorted even if I was to grant her permission."

Shawn quickly stood up in front of her, blocking her exit.

"Of course, I meant to escort her to me aunts' house. Sister Bri – I mean Miss Lawrence, helped me out in my time of need, and all I'm doin' is seekin' to return the favor," he stressed with a nod.

The Superior turned to look out the window at the city below the hill of the convent. Shawn watched her fingers lace behind her back. Finally, after several long minutes of silence, she sat down and invited him to do the same.

"The only way that I would allow you to escort her off of these grounds would be if you were joined in matrimony," she concluded.

He stood quietly still, his mind searching for any other possible solutions to this dilemma.

"I can see by your face that matrimony is not an option," the Mother Superior concluded, though there was a smile hidden in her statement.

"How did you know I worked at the newspaper?" Shawn asked.

"I have my connections, Mr. Fraser. Did you think I would not check into what sort of men work on the convent grounds? Rest assured, I was pleased with the information that I found out."

"So I'm worthy in your eyes, and now you think to marry me off to one of your gils?" he asked flabbergasted.

"No, I'm only dealing with what you have proposed to me of Brianna's situation. I have no doubt that she will remain safe within these walls. It is you, after all, that have extended an invitation, I am only responding to it."

He shook his head, his lips formed a thin straight line. "I've to think on this matter. Do you have the right to make such a decision for Miss Lawrence in her father's stead?"

"Yes. Her father abandoned her here years ago. She's been a charity case ever since. I schooled her out of the kindness of my heart but feel my generosity running out concerning her if she is not to become a nun," she replied simply.

He placed his hat on his head and walked solemnly out the front door without so much as a good-day to you, such was his state of mind. He nearly stumbled down the front steps once outside.

What was he to do? Brianna cared for him when he needed her most. Waited on his every need while convalescing at the convent, and how was he to return her kindness? Walk out on her when she needed him most? Not protect her when that poster clearly stated that the convent would be attacked? He heard the talk of the bricklayers in town. They meant to do more than just burn down the convent the way their threats turned ugly when they spoke of the nuns.

The scene in town with Brianna only made him even more certain that all the nuns at the convent were in jeopardy. *But Brianna wasn't a nun.* That simple fact boggled his mind. She wasn't a nun, but she clearly wanted to be.

He stopped in his tracks at the convent's gate and shook the crazy thoughts from his head. Marry a Catholic, what was he thinking? So, she nursed his wounds, nursing and marrying were two different things.

He jumped onto his horse and rode straight to Murdoch's Pub to distract himself away from his foolish thoughts. Instead, his thoughts were brought back to the convent as soon as he walked inside the tavern and listened to the angry voices of the men around him.

"Skittish as a wild horse, she was. Imagine all that red hair trailing down her back and those big round green eyes looking up at ye. Jus needs the right man to gentle her, calm her, lead her to be the woman God meant her to be. It's unnatural to lock up these women," the barkeep stated.

"'Tis past time to put a stop to the spreading of their poison. Next thing, we'll see our selectman as well as their daughters turn Catholic," the man continued.

"Spreading their deadly toxin, until one day the Pope, himself, will come strolling down Main Street as if he owned the whole damn country!" the man beside him stated.

"Before too long, we'll be rid of the whole lot of them!" another man exclaimed with his glass held high.

Shawn swallowed down the drink in front of him and rode back to the convent. He knew he couldn't leave Brianna at the convent with the information he had hanging like a knife over her head. There was definitely going to be trouble at the convent, with Brianna at the center of it. He needed to get her as far away from it as soon as possible.

He knew enough about the Catholic faith to know that as long as he had no marital relations with Brianna, the church would annul the marriage. When the month of August passed, with all the dangers it held, he would bring her back to the convent to live out her life, and he would go on with his life. His conscience would be relieved, and she could return to her normal life at the convent.

Quickly, he made his way towards the front door of the convent before he changed his mind. His hand was just about to knock on the heavy wooden door when it creaked open. It wasn't the Mother Superior that stood before him, but Brianna.

"Mr. Fraser, Mother told me you wished to speak with me?" Brianna asked, her voice uncertain.

The Superior might have powers beyond us mere humans, he thought to himself.

"Aye, I do, lass, and would ye kindly call me Shawn? I think we know each other well enough to be that familiar with each other, don't ye?"

He walked into the parlor and sat beside her, taking the liberty of placing her hands within his own, now that he had adjusted his thinking to her no longer being an actual nun. She tried to pull her hands free.

"Why do ye struggle so, Brianna?" He enjoyed the feel of her name on his tongue. His aunts were going to love her. *Remember, the marriage will be temporary.*

"Mr. Fraser," she began, then, with a pointed look from him, she stuttered out, "Sh-Shawn, Mother would not approve of this."

He ignored her comment. "Brianna, 'tis a serious question I've come to ask ye. But before that I'd like to say how sorry I am for your loss. I know how much Sister Mary Margaret meant to you."

"She is with the Lord," she said with a sad smile.

"Aye, I'm sure she's lookin' down at us this minute. Now, back to that question I've to ask. Take a deep breath, lass, before I begin.

66

I don't wish ye to faint before ye give me an answer." He watched her eyes grow wide and her body stilled.

It was his turn to have his heart race and his throat squeeze shut. He followed his own instructions and began with a deep breath to ease the sudden tightness in his chest. "I'd like ye to marry me. I've a little money saved up and I'm an honest, hard worker that would take good care of ye."

"Mr. Fraser, I mean, Shawn," she quickly added. "I'm training to be an Ursuline nun. I'm pretty certain that marriage is out of the question."

"I'm sorry to disappoint ye, lass, but yer Superior jus told me herself that ye're no cut out to be a nun. Ye'd be more suited to be a wife and mother." He hated to be so blunt with her, but he felt an urgency to convince her to leave this place before it was too late.

Brianna burst into tears, her hands flying to cover her anguished face. "She just wants," she sniffed, tears running down her cheeks, "to be rid of me ... just like ... father ... left me..!" she stuttered out, each word pulling at his soul. "I told her ... I'd try ... harder! Why won't she ... give me ... a chance ... before sending me ... away?"

She sobbed against his shoulder, her tears melting his heart.

He knew the feeling of abandonment, felt it himself with no parents, growing up with only his two matronly aunts to care for him. He rubbed his chest where it still ached with the loss. He wasn't about to let anything happen to Brianna.

"Brianna, Mother Superior could see as well as I that ye're no suited to this life. Ye must know that in yer own heart. There's much to see out in this world that ye've never laid yer eyes on," Shawn said, warming up to the idea. "First, we'll travel to Halifax, Nova Scotia, for an extended visit with my aunts. You'll love them as they you. Then we'll travel anywhere ye like."

"But what if I don't want to leave this place?" she asked in a timid child-like tone that tore at his heart. He knew he needed to convince her to leave this town for at least the month of August.

"'Tis only temporary, lass. We'll be back soon enough," he consoled.

He could see the stark fear written on her face at the prospect of walking out of this building and off convent grounds, especially after the scene that occurred in town.

His last thought before leaning in towards her, and lifting her face to his, was that he needed to erase her fear the only way he knew how. His lips gently pressed against hers, urging her to relax and think of nothing but his kiss. In the back of his mind, he felt her body soften towards him, a sensation he would not soon forget. He deepened the kiss, his hands smoothly framing her face, making him forget where they both sat until a familiar cough interrupted his concentration.

"Mother!" shrieked Brianna, jumping out of her seat and away from him. Shawn watched her face turn several shades of red.

"I see you've made the right choice, Brianna," her Superior announced in her no-nonsense way. "A nun would never have responded to a man that way," she assured her. When the color of Brianna's face deepened further with embarrassment, she added, "You must follow the path that God has set out for you."

Shawn hated the way her Superior so bluntly threw the facts of her actions before her, making her feel more uncomfortable.

He hated pressing her for an answer, but time was of the essence. He bent his knees to level his eyes with hers. "Is that a yes, lass?"

When she nodded woodenly, her face blank of emotion, he gathered her stiff body into his arms. He knew he pressured her to agree to marry him, but he ignored the simple fact, knowing that he would be keeping her from harm by taking her out of this convent.

"Then, it is decided. I will have Father McBrien come up and perform the ceremony on Sunday," the Superior announced.

Now it was his turn to blanch. The decision to marry was one thing, but the idea of his own father actually performing the ceremony was another.

"The sooner the better," the Superior reminded him with a pointed look in his direction.

"Of course, this Sunday service, I mean mass will be fine," he replied, clearing his mind. He wasn't about to reveal the fact that he was a Protestant to the Mother Superior and make ruin of his marriage plans. She would no doubt change her carefully thought-out plans and find another candidate to marry Brianna. And the thought of that irritated him more than he cared to admit.

They sat, two opposing forces across from each other, father to son, a mirrored reflection, young to old. Shawn despised the similarities, hated receiving anything from him, even the things he had no control over.

He kept his voice deceptively calm, covering his growing irritation. "What do ye mean, ye refuse to marry us? Ye have no right."

"I have every right. Brianna is a kind, innocent girl, who has had enough hardship in her life. She doesn't deserve to be a pawn in whatever plan you have concocted to get back at me," his father stated, his voice rising with emotion.

"I'm marrying her, whether ye do it or not," Shawn replied stubbornly, crossing his arms.

"Her only wish in life is to remain at the convent. Are you going to take that away from her too?" his father exclaimed, hands flying into the air.

Shawn stood up, his patience thinning. "I'm not ye, *father*," he said with disgust. "I've no intention of harmin' the gil."

"The Reverend Mother told me of your reputation as a writer, pretty impressive for a man of such young age. Why not leave here, go on with your life elsewhere? There's no need to bring Brianna into this. If your thirst for revenge runs so deep, have the courage to aim it at the true source, not her. Tell all what I did to your mother. Expose my sins, I deserve no less from you," he urged.

"In time, ye'll pay. My marriage has nothing to do with that."

"Is there nothing I can do to change your mind?" The desperation in his voice was beginning to grate on Shawn's nerves.

"The church supported your sordid behavior and made my mother the scapegoat. I've got good reason to hate you as well as your church."

His father's eyes widened in shock. "Then you're not even Catholic?"

"Aye," Shawn stated with a lift of his chin.

His father stood across from him. "I cannot with a clear conscience perform the ceremony. I can't do this to Brianna."

Anger and frustration twisted inside of Shawn. His patience strained to the limit. "This is utterly ridiculous. Who are ye to judge?

Look at your own life filled with secrets. At least I care for the lass and am willin' to marry her. 'Tis more than I can say ye did for my own mother!" His fist slammed down hard on the table between them.

Silence echoed against the walls of the room. His father slowly sank back down into his chair, his eyes a hollow of pain. Shawn heaved a deep, irritated sigh.

Into the awkward silence, Shawn said, "The convent is going to be attacked. 'Tis not a matter of if but when. The Reverend Mother doesn't heed the threats. These men won't stop until they're allowed inside the convent with or without the Superior's permission. Everyone inside the convent will be in danger, especially Brianna."

His father shook his head, clearly disconcerted. "Your concern is truly with Brianna?"

"Why does that surprise you? I am my mother's son."

Shawn stationed himself behind the back fence of the convent that night as soon as darkness fell. He wasn't going to take any chances with anything happening before Sunday when he would be able to take Brianna safely away from here.

He was used to this sort of work, staking out a subject, waiting for something to happen. It was only a few hours later, to his surprise, a shadowy figure made its way from the convent toward the back fence. The person wore a long flowing gown with hood covering over her head, making only the face visible to his eyes, but even that was undistinguishable in the pitch-dark surroundings of the night.

"Allow me." He extended his hand in a helpful gesture to boost the person over the fence. When he heard her startled gasp, he berated himself for his clumsy appearance. What was he thinking, scaring the lass? Was he losing his touch?

She took a couple steps back away from him. He couldn't believe his luck, a runaway nun. Now, this would be a story to satisfy his hungry boss.

"If ye wish to leave, I'll help ye," he encouraged in a loud whisper. If anything, he didn't want to frighten the poor girl more than he had already. "Jus take me hand."

She stood frozen before him.

"I couldn't … sleep, thought … stroll … help," she stuttered in reply.

The sound of her voice startled him. He leaned over the fence to get a closer look at her face, then noticed the few strands of red hair slip down into the moonlight.

"Brianna?!" he burst out shocked. Quickly, he made his way over the fence and toward her before she could make her way back into the building. His arm grabbed her shoulder, stopping her.

"What are ye doing?!" he exclaimed while she struggled to free his grip.

"If ye wished to leave the convent earlier, ye only had to tell me," he stated. When she didn't answer him, he continued, voicing his thoughts aloud, "It's me ye wish to avoid, isn't it, lass?"

She turned her face away from him, remaining silent.

"Brianna, if it's freedom ye want, I'll give it to ye … right after we're wedded. I've a debt to pay in yer regard." When she looked up at him confused, he thought quickly, knowing she had little choice in the matter and said, "I've a need for a wife in name only. I'm constantly badgered by mothers shoving their eligible daughters my way. Marriage would end all that."

"I should think so," she said indignantly.

"I'll bring ye to my aunts' house in Halifax for an extended holiday. After a month passes, I'll return ye to the convent. I give ye me word."

"You promise?" she asked quietly.

"Aye, if nothing else, I'm an honest man," he replied, "But answer me one question before ye return. Are ye the nun that jumped the fence a few weeks back?"

"Which part of the fence?" she asked, uncertain.

"I don't believe it," he murmured right before she turned and ran back the way she came, never once looking back.

CHAPTER SEVEN

Shawn shifted his long legs uncomfortably in the close quarters of the stagecoach. He turned to look out the small window beside him while he toyed with the unfamiliar gold band that sat on his finger.

Brianna slept on his shoulder, her fearful eyes now resting peacefully. The quick wedding ceremony performed by his father late last night was quick and efficient. Within a matter of minutes, the deed was done and he escorted Brianna out of the convent and into the waiting stagecoach. She cried on his shoulder all night long. Finally, to his relief, in the wee hours of the morning, she fell asleep.

Shawn glanced down at her sleeping form. His hands gently smoothed her hair away from her troubled face and attempted to wake her from the grips of a nightmare.

"Bri, wake up."

He watched her eyes open, then startle, once she realized she had been sleeping in his arms. When she went to move away, his arms kept her securely tucked against his side.

"Do ye want to talk about it?" he gently urged. When she looked away from him, his finger guided her face back up to his.

Frustrated, he added, "I know the ceremony last night was quick but legal. I'm yer husband, and I want ye to trust me."

Tears pooled in her eyes.

"I know ye didn't want to leave the convent, but like I promised to ye earlier, ye'd be my wife in name only. So there's no reason why we can't be friends, is there?"

She shook her head, her face serious, her deep green eyes somber when she looked at him. "You promise you won't be mad at me?" she asked softly.

"Of course, lass, my only wish is to see ye happy."

"I miss the convent, and the Reverend Mother, and Sister Mary Louise, the children, and, of course, Sister Mary Margaret. I really miss her," she stated, promptly bursting into tears again.

72

His heart squeezed painfully. He knew he did the right thing removing her from the convent, but he hated how miserable she felt. "'Tis for the better as ye shall see once ye meet the aunts. They're goin' to take a fancy to ye and rightly so. Ye'll love Halifax. And if ye wish to return to the convent after a period of time, ye'll be free to do so, jus as I promised."

His fingers wiped the tears that fell from her watery green eyes. She deserved a lush wedding ceremony with all the trimmings, as every young bride should have. The Superior, however, didn't want the town's people to hear of the marriage and assume things that were not true. He agreed to a hushed ceremony, since the people's attitude in town had grown worse, and he didn't wish to add to the idle gossip.

Shawn checked his timepiece. He sent a message earlier to his old friend, explaining his need to sail up the coast from the harbor town north of Boston. He only hoped the message reached him in time.

When the wharf came into sight, his apprehension grew. The sailors that walked along the dock craved female companionship after long, lonely weeks at sea. Numerous pubs lined the street opposite the docks, catering to the sailors' thirst for drink and women. His hand patted the holster of his gun.

"Stay close, Bri. The men workin' the docks aren't the best sort." He worried more after he looked down at her simple white dress. The thin fabric sensuously skimmed over the feminine curves of her delicate body, making him wish that he had a cape to cover every inch of her. The month, he realized, would be long and arduous to endure with his wife's alluring body tempting him each day.

He helped her down out of the coach and made his way across the street, relieved to see his good friend Robert McAndry's ship there.

McAndry had given him the male companionship he sorely needed growing up with two doting women. The elderly man took him under his wing, protecting him from harm and teaching him a thing or two about life.

McAndry stood on the deck of his ship, his tall form stoically bracing against the sea breeze. His dark hair, gone an unfamiliar gray, proved it had been quite a while since he sailed home onboard his ship.

"Good to see ye, lad." His old friend patted him affectionately on the back, then turned to look behind him. "Is that her?" he asked, his eyes squinting at Brianna's distant form.

Shawn spun around, his heart in his throat. His eyes flew to Brianna standing in the center of a group of ruffians, conversing with them as if she were at a social gathering. He strode quickly over to her.

Brianna tried to keep up with Shawn's long stride, but ultimately, she was left in the dust behind him. She didn't mind, since it gave her a moment to soak in the sights, never before seeing such grand sailing ships except in the books she read.

She breathed in the salty air filled with the smell of freshly caught fish. Her body reveled in the ocean's breeze that tugged at her hat, swirled her dress, and loosened tendrils of hair from her braid to dance in the wind. She wanted to sing out a hundred verses of Alleluia's to the glorious endless blue-green of the ocean as it stretched across the horizon.

"Quite a sight, ain't it now?" a short stocky man stated, standing beside her.

She nodded, not quite sure if she could speak over the lump in her throat, the vastness of God's glory leaving her speechless. She didn't want to turn her eyes away from the blue but she also didn't wish to be rude to the man beside her. She shifted a quick glance his way, noticing the loose-fitting clothes of a sailor, dark tanned skin on an elderly face and kind blue eyes that glanced back at her from beneath white bushy brows.

"I remember my first time like it was yesterday," the aged sailor began with a smile and a twinkle in his eye.

"Aye, I'm sure you do!" another sailor stated, slapping the older man on the back. "Colby, aren't you going to introduce me to the sweet thing beside you, or are ya keeping this catch all to yourself?" he laughed.

"Pay no mind to this ruffian. He's the manners of a sea lion and the smell of one too!" the elderly sailor laughed. "I'm Jack Colby, ma'am. And this is Tommy Stuart."

A group of men gathered around her, friends of the elderly sailor,

74

and for some odd reason, she didn't feel anxious. Instead of fear, she felt comfort in her newly found friends.

One, with jet-black hair to the length of his shoulders, elbowed Mr. Colby before she had the chance to properly introduce herself. "Jack, where have ya been hiding this red siren? Sail the seas with me, love, or at least join me for dinner," he asked with a broad wink directed at her.

She ignored the flirtatious man and turned to Mr. Colby. "It is good to meet you, sir. My name is Brianna Lawrence Fraser."

Shawn shoved her behind him, shielding her with his huge frame. "Didn't I tell ye to stay close?" he hissed quietly out of the side of his mouth.

"What's the matter?" she asked. "These men are only being friendly." Her head peeked out from behind him and smiled back at Mr. Colby so that he wouldn't be hurt by her husband's bad behavior.

"This woman's me wife," he warned, "And I'll slit the throat of any man that harms her." He was glad that the men scattered at his words. He didn't want to spill blood in front of his new wife.

"Wasn't that a bit harsh?" she whispered over to him. "They were all being hospitable, even inviting me to have dinner with them."

He escorted her to McAndry's ship, holding her securely to his side. "Trust me, those men aren't in the least bit hospitable. They only have one thing on their mind and it's not food."

"Robert McAndry, at yer service, lass." McAndry bowed low before Brianna. His hand came up to pat Shawn on the inside of his jacket. "Ye'll need to pack that gun wherever ye venture with a wife as beautiful as that," he remarked, then winked at Brianna. A gold tooth sparkled from within his wide smile.

"You've a gun?" Brianna asked, her eyes widening at the sight. She realized how little she knew about her new husband. She'd need to discuss it with him in private the first chance she got.

"Come away with ye, then. I'll show ye to yer cabin," Captain McAndry stated. He escorted her onboard the ship and to his cabin.

"We're no goin' to take yer cabin from ye," Shawn announced.

"'Tis me weddin' present to ye, that and passage north, so don't make a fuss, laddie. I've known ye since ye were a wee lad, so don't go thinkin' jus because ye're built bigger and taller now than these old bones that ye can tell me what I can or cannot do. Enjoy." Captain McAndry strode out of the room whistling.

Not more than a minute had passed before Shawn stated, "I've our chests to help board." Her new husband turned and nearly ran out of the room before she had a chance to reply.

She dropped her body onto the captain's bed and wept. Her father thought her a nuisance, so he left her at a convent never to return. Mother Superior married her off to the first man that asked just to get rid of her. And her new husband married her only to repay a debt that he felt he owed her. She knew he couldn't wait to drop her off at his relations in Halifax and never see her again.

Hours passed. At dark, a soft knock sounded on her door. The captain's voice spoke to her from the other side, interrupting her bout of weeping.

"Mrs. Fraser, I wish to invite ye to dine with me tonight. I'll send a lad to escort ye to me table when ye're ready."

She wiped her eyes with the back of her hand and answered the captain without opening the door. "Thank you, sir. I'll be ready shortly."

She'd rather stay in her cabin all night and sob about her woeful life, drench herself in anguish, rather than sit at a dinner table and make polite conversation.

Mother would advice her to put the captain's feelings before her own. She wouldn't want to offend him by refusing his kind invitation. Her husband, on the other hand, had left her to fend for herself. Therefore, she breathed in deeply, reined in her emotions, smoothed out the wrinkles on her traveling gown, and waited for her escort.

As soon as she walked into the dining room, she was surprised to see her husband deep in conversation with the captain. All discussion stopped when she entered the room.

Captain McAndry jumped up from his seat and slid out a chair for her. "Did you find your accommodations comfortable, Mrs. Fraser?"

"Yes, thank you."

"The food is simple aboard ship but generously given. I hope the voyage will be pleasant for you," the captain added.

"I'm sure it will be. Thank you, Captain," she replied, careful not to glance at her husband beside her.

She immediately bowed her head in prayer as soon as she sat down, her finger automatically forming the sign of the cross at the end of her silent prayer before beginning her meal.

"Catholic." Captain McAndry didn't ask but stated the fact, then glanced at her new husband with one eyebrow raised high in question. Her husband looked away uncomfortably. The captain slapped Shawn on the back with a laugh. Brianna looked at both of them confused.

Captain McAndry ignored her confusion. "So, how does it feel to be married to such a noted newspaper reporter?"

"A reporter?" Her eyes glanced at her new husband's averted eyes, and she realized she really didn't know anything about him. No, she was wrong, she did know one thing about him – her husband was a liar, which only made her more distressed. What other secrets did he keep hidden?

"Captain, will you please excuse me? I find that I'm not feeling well right now." Brianna stood to leave, surprised that Shawn, also, stood and accompanied her back to their cabin in silence.

Once they both entered the room, she swiftly turned around. "Why did you pretend to the Reverend Mother that you were a groundskeeper? You lied, Shawn, after you told me if nothing else you were an honest man."

"Bri, we've agreed to keep this marriage in name only, no commitments between us, except for the ones on paper. There's a number of reasons why I can't explain the facts of my employment to ye. Ye've got to trust me on that," he stated into the quiet of the room.

"You don't like me, do you?" Her hand fluttered up to her hair nervously. Her eyes stared down at the floor.

He crossed the room toward her in two strides, gathering her body in his arms. "Quite the opposite, lass," he whispered into her ear. He tugged the pins from her hair, freeing the long red locks to fall loosely down her back. "Hasn't anyone ever told ye how beautiful ye are?"

77

She shook her head against his shoulder.

"It's a sin to be vain," she whispered.

She felt him laugh softly against her neck.

"My sweet, Bri, will I ever get used to yer virtuous nature?"

His lips showered her with kisses on her cheeks, eyes, and nose, drinking in the simple innocence of her, lingering over each sweet taste of her skin. When his lips swayed over to her mouth, delving into the velvety softness of them, he knew he needed to stop. He took a deep breath at the sound of her sensuous sigh, stretched out his arms stiffly in front of him, and physically stepped away from her body.

"Does that answer yer question?" he asked before striding out of the room.

Shawn slammed open the door into McAndry's room and sat down heavily on a chair at the table, his mood sour.

McAndry sat opposite him at the table, a slight grin on his face.

"So, Catholic gil, is she?" His old friend slapped him on the back and placed a shot of whiskey on the table.

Shawn took a long drink of the liquid.

"I had a feelin' ye'd be needin' that. What got into ye, lad? Marryin' a gil of the faith ye vowed ye'd hate 'til the day ye died?" McAndry asked exasperated.

"'Tis a long story."

Shawn stood and paced the small cabin floor that McAndry bunked in for the journey, his large body feeling claustrophobic in the small space.

"Aye, and 'tis a long night. Hard not to notice the red-rimmed eyes of the poor sad lass. My days are limited, lad, so start talkin' quick," McAndry urged.

With his sour mood, even McAndry's dark humor didn't affect him.

"I met her investigatin' a convent for wrongdoin's," he began, giving a pointed look to the old man not to say a word. At his nod, Shawn continued.

"Me boss, desperate to take down the Catholic church, and unbeknownst to me, had me roughed up a bit and dropped outside the convent gates to get me inside to investigate the story. Bri found me bruised and beaten and nursed me back to health. I owed her a debt of gratitude for that," he stated.

McAndry interrupted, "Enough to marry her?"

Shawn stopped his pacing. "Aye."

"I may be an old sea dog, but I know when there's somethin' missin' from a tale. What is it, lad?"

"Her life was in danger," Shawn stated.

"Danger in a convent?" McAndry asked, one brow lifted high in disbelief.

Shawn hesitated, then went back to his pacing.

McAndry grew impatient and spat, "Out with it, lad."

"There's papers posted throughout Charlestown warning the selectmen to investigate the convent for wrongdoings or they would take matters in their own hands," Shawn began.

"Is that all this is about? I've heard talk against the Catholics for ages now. You told me most of it."

Shawn turned a chair around and sat down on it. He stretched his long legs out to ease the tension out of them. "The only way the Superior would let Brianna leave the convent with me was if I married her," Shawn stated, his mind still reeling from the simple fact that he was a married man. He shook off the uncomfortable feelings, reminding himself that the marriage was temporary.

"'Tis only a matter of time until these men in town crash through the convent doors."

Shawn watched his old friend guzzle down an entire cup of whiskey then slowly raise his dark eyes to him.

"Now, lad, it all makes sense, but there's one thing that still confuses me. When did ye fall in love with the lass?" McAndry asked.

Shawn shook off his friend's absurd words, worrying more about the month to come. How would he endure an entire month with such an alluring wife?

Shawn unlatched the gate to the fence in front of a small farmhouse. He allowed her to enter before him. Flowering vines covered the front of the building while overgrown bushes of lilacs and hydrangeas fought for space along the ground. They had just started down the small stone pathway lined with purple speckled violets, when the front door flew open unexpectedly.

The short round figures of two elderly women came rushing toward her new husband with all the fervor of two young girls. Shawn had described them to perfection. Aunt Liddea, a few years older than Bea, looked more reserved than her sister, with her hair severely pulled into a tight knot at the back of her head, although her heart shone in her eyes when she first spotted Shawn. Aunt Bea, with her golden brown hair pulled loosely into a bun, smiled warmly at Shawn.

"You've come for a visit, have ye?" Aunt Bea asked, hurrying into Shawn's arms.

"Shame on ye for not at least warnin' us a little! We could've had all your favorites warmin' in the oven, waitin' for ya!" Aunt Liddea scolded.

After they finished their welcome with *their* Shawn, they both fell silent and turned their surprised eyes to her. She waited for her new husband to properly introduce her.

"You've brought a nun to visit with us?" Aunt Liddea remarked, her eyes traveling the length of her gown.

Shawn cleared his throat and looked to be a tad uncomfortable when he replied, "She's no nun, she's me wife." He stated the words softly, his brogue heavily accented.

"A wife!" they both burst out at the same time. Brianna had the urge to step back and away.

"Ye've frightened her," Shawn reprimanded.

"I'm sorry, dear, it's just that, well, we never thought...." Aunt Bea began.

He turned to Brianna. "What my aunts are sayin' is that they never thought a scalawag like me would ever settle down."

"What's a scalawag?" Brianna asked.

"Oh dear," the two aunts said in unison, glancing at each other. They linked their arms with Brianna. "Come with us, we've much to explain. Where have ye been keepin' yourself, locked up in a convent?" They both glanced down at her outfit again and laughed at their humor.

When they noticed that neither Shawn nor she smiled, their laughter died. They both turned to Shawn, their eyes stern when they demanded, "You've much to explain, Shawn Fraser. If you've gotten this poor young thing in trouble, a woman of the cloth no less – God protect yer soul!"

"Lower yer voices, ye're makin' a scene for yer neighbors. I'll do the explainin' inside, if ye don't mind," he declared, walking past the women and into the house.

He stopped halfway to the house, turned around, his good manners clicking in. "*Mrs. Fraser*," he emphasized, "this is my Aunt Bea and my Aunt Liddea." That stated, he strode into the door of the house.

"He was always a handful that one," Aunt Liddea said, shaking her head.

"Aye, but we raised him the best we could, sister," Aunt Bea consoled.

"Ladies!" they heard Shawn shout from the door.

"He never liked dilly-dallying our Shawn. Always one to get to the meat of things and forge on," they said, walking into the house and down the hall to the kitchen.

Shawn turned her toward the stairs as soon as she entered the house. "Bri, why don't ye go on up the stairs and rest a bit. My room is the first on the left, make yerself comfortable. I'm sure ye're exhausted." It was more of an order than a request, but she *was* too tired to argue.

Both aunts stood with their arms crossed before Shawn.

"No, she wasn't a nun, not even one in trainin', not really anyway," he began.

"She's Catholic?" Aunt Liddea asked.

"Catholic," Aunt Bea echoed before he had a chance to answer. Her eyes were wide with shock.

He gave a curt nod. "She has lived in the Ursuline convent since she was a little gil and looked up to the nuns there, especially the Mother Superior. Her father abandoned her there years ago. The nuns schooled her ever since. The Mother Superior became her guardian."

"Poor little thing, how sad," they voiced in unison.

"Yes, well, I met her at the convent one day and grew to like her, so I married her," he announced to their expectant faces.

"That's it? Ye grew to *like* her? Aren't ye madly in love with her?" Aunt Bea asked.

"Why else would he marry a Catholic gil?" Aunt Liddea replied, her eyes narrowing. The two of them placed their hands on their hips and shot him looks that would kill a lesser man.

"Ladies, ye know me better than that. She's an innocent and is goin' to remain that way. I am not my father!" He strode out of the kitchen, ignoring the surprised looks on both of his interfering aunts' faces.

A shuffling noise in the middle of the night woke him up from the corner chair on which he was sleeping. Brianna's slim form lightly trod across the floor of the bedroom toward the door. He called out to her softly so as not to alarm her if she was asleep. When she didn't answer, curiosity had him following her down the darkened stairwell and into the kitchen.

Ah, she was hungry, he thought to himself. He reached for a lamp on the way and lit it walking into the kitchen.

Before the wick was thoroughly lit, she turned around and dropped to the floor before him. She stood on her knees, her head bowed, mumbling, "Please forgive me."

At first, he stood there stunned, not knowing what to do. When he did come to his senses, he quickly took her by the arm and lifted her off the floor.

He shook her arm lightly, hoping to awaken her.

"Brianna, 'tis Shawn, yer husband," he said gruffly.

He placed the lamp on the table beside them and ushered her to a chair. "Were ye dreamin', Bri?"

"I'm sorry, I thought you were Mother, and well, I shouldn't be out of bed in the middle of the night without permission. The last time this happened I walked out of–" she began, then stopped, her cheeks bright with color.

"Go on," he urged.

She shook her head. "The Reverend Mother made me promise not to ever make mention of it again."

"Jus nod if I'm correct," Shawn ventured. "Did ye sleepwalk several weeks ago?" He waited for her to nod in agreement like he guessed she would. "Did ye climb over the fence and walk to the neighbor's house all while ye were asleep?"

Her eyes filled with tears. "The man thought I was crazed, my bloody body scratched and torn from the thorny rose bushes and fence I tumbled over in my sleep. He found me lying on his front step, asleep." She slapped a hand over her mouth. Could she never learn to obey?

"And the night before our wedding?" he asked.

She nodded again. "Mother says that I bury my worries instead of lifting them up to God in prayer. I don't know why I do it, I just do. I was so glad that you awoke me that night at the convent before I wandered off and disgraced the convent once again. I've tried to make it up to Mother but–" she said, her hands falling limply to her sides.

Obviously, the Mother Superior cared enough about her not to disclose the serious threat against the convent because of her innocent sleepwalking. Or maybe she knew the people in town would never believe or rather would never want to believe such a simple explanation.

"Bri, ye're not in a convent anymore, me aunts can confess to that. There's no rules to be broken here," he added gently.

He brushed her unruly mop of hair away from her fearful eyes. It all made sense to him now. She didn't knowingly leave the convent that she loved. Her sleepwalking took her over the fence and away from the convent. She couldn't control what she did in her sleep anymore than he could. That's why he slept in the chair and not the bed, he thought with a grimace.

It irked him that her Superior had somehow turned the situation around and placed blame on Brianna's shoulders by keeping her quiet. He longed to wipe the look of fear permanently off her face. The poor girl was racked with guilt for numerous things – all of which were no fault of hers. She needed to have fun, live her life to its fullest. This month, he would make certain of that.

He rubbed his hands together. "I was thinkin' of makin' one of me famous bread omelets. Are ye hungry, lass?" The last time they ate was on the ship this morning.

She nodded her head shyly.

"There should be no secrets between us, if ye're hungry come out and say it. Ye're my wife, aren't ye?" he stated, one eyebrow raised high in question.

"Temporarily, yes," she quietly replied.

Now, it was his turn to feel uncomfortable. He knew to what she was referring. "Bri, there's things that ye don't know about me that need to be said." And some things that needed to remain unsaid for now at least.

She rose slowly from her chair, her face bright red when she stood bravely before him and said into the quiet of the kitchen, "It's me, isn't it?"

She was a luring sight standing there, lamplight framing her curves, only a thin cotton nightdress covering the length of her body. He was tempted to forget his good intentions and give in to the need that burned inside him.

His conscience, on the other hand, reminded him that to do so would not be fair to her. He knew Brianna might not want to have anything to do with him after he explained about himself and the work he did at the convent. He married her only to repay a debt and ease his conscience, he reminded himself, not to satisfy his own lustful cravings. As long as she remained pure, she could go back to the convent.

He cleared his throat uncomfortably. "As much as I'm tempted, Bri, I think yer stomach needs fillin' first."

She turned so quickly that she nearly tipped over the lantern on the table.

"Bri, try to understand, I'm thinkin' of ye, lass," he stated to her back, his hand rubbing lightly up and down her arms.

She nodded awkwardly and sat back down. He could see the effort that it took for her to tuck away the hurt he made her feel. She even forced a smile on her face for his sake and said, "I *am* starved and would love some of those bread omelets."

"Ye're goin' to love them! Now, if I can find some breadcrumbs in here. Give me a couple minutes and I'll be right back." He lit a lantern and headed out to the barn to get a little milk for the omelet and a couple of eggs.

Uneasiness settled over him. It first began when they disembarked from the ship, impatiently watching Brianna say her good-byes to the entire crew of men – all of which, to his irritation, she knew on a first name basis. Now, he glanced over his shoulder, his eyes searching into the morning mist, seeing nothing but sensing someone nearby. He patted the holster on his waist.

CHAPTER EIGHT

Brianna lifted her face into the wind, its fiery force whipping strands of hair against her face. Her arms tightened around her husband's chest, sitting side-saddle upon the horse, forcing her to forget her inhibitions in fear of falling off the majestic creature.

Shawn sat snuggly behind her, expertly guiding the sleek jet-black horse up steep trails, across creeks, and down narrow pathways, while she sat with eyes shut tight, hands gripping his waist.

When he finally pulled back on the reins of the horse, her curiosity made her squint one eye open, only to gasp in awe at the view before her. They stood upon a plateau, overlooking lush mountains rolling in green, stretched out across a horizon as far as her eyes could see. Meadows of wildflowers painted the hills surrounding them.

Brianna breathed in the sweet fragrance and sighed deeply. "How did you ever leave all this?"

"As a young lad, I needed to see the world before I could appreciate this beauty. I found out quick enough, though, especially in the cities, that beauty like this is not found all over."

She laughed, surprising herself and causing her mood to turn melancholy. "This reminds me of the beautiful gardens at the convent."

"Give it time, lass. I brought ye here to boost yer spirits. I've always had a need to come to this very spot every time I make a trip back home."

"I've a need of my own," she replied with a girlish giggle.

Before Shawn knew what she was about to do, she slid down from the tall horse and ran toward the meadow of flowers, her hands stretched out wide, touching the tips of the flowers she passed.

An overwhelming desire came over her to be in the middle of it all, touch it, roll around in it. She let her body fall backwards into the abundance of blooms.

"Are ye all right, Bri?" Shawn asked, running over to her, his eyes filled with worry.

Brianna tilted her head up above the stems of flowers, a wide grin on her face. "Yes, more than all right! God has graced this place with such beauty that I wanted to feel its lushness all around me!"

Shawn sat down beside her, laughing. "Watchin' ye view the world for the first time is the most pleasant of sights."

She grinned back at him, then grew serious. "I thought that I never wanted to leave the convent, but then I would have missed all this. Thank you for showing me."

He grew thoughtful. "Did ye enjoy yer life at the convent? The nun that escaped two years ago told all sorts of tales."

"I overheard some of my teachers at school talk about the young nun when she disappeared, but I didn't know her. I do know how difficult it can be to follow the rules of St. Ursula. I'd guess that any nun might feel the need to leave the convent rather than face disgrace at failing."

"Is that how ye felt, lass, that night I spied ye makin' yer way over the fence of the convent?"

"I was confused," she replied, closing her eyes, a rosy glow painting her cheeks.

The simple fact that he was forced to marry her in order for him to take her out of the convent for a short length of time was enough of a story to write to spur the already angered people of Charlestown, if he so deemed.

"When you broke a rule, what happened?" he asked, intrigued by her honesty.

"I'd be punished," she replied matter-of-factly.

"How would ye be punished?"

"I'd be told to string rosary beads, kneel and recite scripture, certain chores of ironing, all sorts of different things that the Reverend Mother felt would help me in my devotion to God to be a better Catholic. I appreciated every penance given so that my sins would be forgiven."

"Aye, there's some that would say only God can forgive sins," Shawn commented.

"The Reverend Mother is like the Holy Mother of God on this earth," Brianna replied as if he were stupid.

"In yer eyes only, lass. How often did Father McBrien or any other priest come to visit at the convent?"

She gave him an odd look before she answered. "The priest visited often to work in the garden, other priests came to say mass in our chapel too. Why do you ask?"

"I'll be honest with ye, Bri. There was talk in town that the priests did more than say mass, much more."

"I'm not sure what you're saying?" Brianna asked, confused.

"I heard talk that there were nuns locked in the cellar of the building – pregnant nuns," he added, his jaw clenched.

"What!" she exclaimed. "Why would you say such a horrendous thing?!"

"Whoa, I'm just tellin' ye what I heard."

"Is that why you wanted to see the cellar at the convent?" she asked, crossing her arms tightly against her body.

"I won't lie to ye, Bri. I wanted to see for myself the truth of the matter."

She jabbed her finger at his chest. "You were investigating the convent the whole time you stayed there? I don't understand. Your bruises were real. How could you fake that?"

He pushed her finger away. "The bruises were real, I've still the ache time and again, but they were inflicted by men my boss hired to get me inside the convent."

Shawn watched her eyes grow wide before narrowing when she spoke. "So the whole time I cared for you, nursed your wounds, you lied to me and used me to try to get information on the convent for the sake of a story?" Brianna asked, her anger beginning to twist into tiny knots inside her. She felt utterly betrayed by a man she thought she knew.

"Aye, and before ye ask the question – Mother Superior knew all about what I was doing. She allowed me to do my job because, as I later realized, she had nothing to hide and wished me to see that," he replied.

"Is this what you wanted to talk to me about earlier or is there something else I should know about you?" she asked, her hands fidgeting at her waist.

He hesitated before he spoke, not wanting to upset her further, but feeling the need to be honest with her. "Only the fact that I'm not Catholic and never wish to be," he blurted out to her stunned face.

When she said nothing, he added, "I told ye before, I needed a wife *in name only*, yer religion makes no difference to me," he lied. "And mine should make no difference to ye."

"You're Protestant?" she stuttered out as if it was a crime.

"Yes, does that offend you?" he snapped back at her, harsher than he meant. She flinched at his tone of voice, which only made him feel worse.

"I wish to return to the convent as soon as possible," she managed to whisper, sliding her eyes shut, but not before Shawn glimpsed the hurt he placed in them.

"As soon as the month has passed, ye'll be free to return to the convent. I'll escort ye there myself," he promised.

They both sat in stony silence, lost in their own thoughts. Until Brianna sat straight up, a silly grin forming on her face.

"It looks as if ye've jus dipped into the communion wine."

She ignored his comment. "Of course, this all makes sense now. Mother didn't care if you were a Protestant or not because this marriage was only a way for me to experience the secular world before she granted me the black veil. She probably thought it educational for me to experience a different religion as well," Brianna added. "I don't know why I didn't think of this earlier."

Shawn didn't have the heart to tell her that her Reverend Mother had no such thing in mind, quite the opposite. She never mentioned the idea of Brianna *ever* returning to the convent. If Brianna wanted to return, he would do everything in his power to persuade the Mother Superior to take her back after the month of August had passed into September.

The green of her eyes darkened, her face serious when she stated, "And I'd never touch the holy wine. I've seen the results of such an indulgence."

At the word *indulgence* his senses became alert, his fingers tingled. As calmly as he could, he asked, "Indulgence of wine?"

Brianna looked away quickly, realizing her slip of tongue.

Shawn grabbed her by the shoulders. "If Father McBrien drank too much and took advantage of ye – I've a right to know. I am your husband!"

She slapped his hands away. "How dare you accuse dear old Father McBrien of such a thing! He's such a kind man and has never ever done anything untoward."

"If not him, then another priest that visited the monastery," he persisted.

Her voice broke when she stated, "Mother must have been too upset the day Sister Mary Margaret died to realize how much wine she drank. I found her half asleep behind the barn, an empty wine bottle beside her."

Shawn struggled to keep the excitement out of his voice. "Did anyone else see the Reverend Mother like that?"

"No, I helped her back to her room. She asked me never to speak of it again. I didn't until now. I just wanted you to understand that Father McBrien is a good man," she repeated, in case he didn't hear her the first time she said it.

She was right, his mind wasn't on her words any longer. The information she gave him was exactly what he needed to close down Mount Benedict Academy as well as the nunnery. Parents would pull their daughters out of a school administered by an inebriated nun.

With the temperance movement gaining popularity these days, this story would race across the nation. Newspapers as far as California would run his story on a drunken Superior running a school of Protestant girls – it made good news.

This was it – the story he waited for all his life to exact the revenge for his mother's death. This was too good to be true. He patted his pockets for paper to begin and realized Brianna still sat beside him. He nearly forgot her in all his excitement!

She turned her head away from him, clearly upset. "Would you mind taking me back to your aunts' house, I'm suddenly feeling tired."

He didn't believe her. And as much as he longed to sit with pen and ink and write down the story, he didn't want to leave her company. "Aye, I do mind. This holiday was for ye to experience the secular world, and ye cannot do that from inside my aunts' cottage.

Come," Shawn stated, giving her a hand up off the ground. "There's a ceilidh down the road, which would be the perfect place for ye to experience something new," he announced, lifting her light frame onto his horse, then saddling up behind her. He'd write down her words later in the evening while she slept.

"A what?"

"A kay-lee, 'tis a gathering of all the Scottish families in the area. There's food, dancing and all sorts of games to play."

She sat primly in front of him; her hands encircling the saddle horn, nose tilted up with disdain. With a smile, he grabbed hold of the harness of the horse, secured his arms around her, and kicked him into movement. He struggled not to laugh when she turned toward him and clung onto his waist, forgetting her anger.

"Are you trying to kill us?" she yelled into the wind, her long hair twisting and turning in the air around them.

"What?" Shawn replied, feigning deafness.

He reveled in the feel of her warm body snuggled up against him. His arms encircled her, keeping her securely on top of the horse, knowing that the distraction would help keep his mind off the information he had obtained.

The fields by the McGillry farm were filled with wagons, horses, and children. Shawn rode into the area, tipping his hat to friends he hadn't seen in a few years, their hands full of wives and children. He was glad that he decided to bring Brianna here. A ceilidh was just the type of fun he'd like to share with her.

He had waited years to write a story to discredit the Catholic religion, a few hours would make no difference.

Groups of men gathered with bagpipes practicing their tunes, while young girls tossed and kicked their legs up high to the rhythm of music. He leaned toward Brianna's widened eyes, watching her shift from one activity to the next.

Shawn squeezed her hand. "The Scotts are good people, I can vouch for that. Let's tie this horse up and wander around a bit, see who's here."

She held tightly to his hand while he led her through fields of tents and people. The smell of roasting meat filled the air and raucous laughter accompanied by the sweet scent of whiskey.

Children ran in and out of family tents, giggling and playing, ignoring the reprimands of their parents. He didn't realize how much he missed all of this until now.

"Shawn Fraser, have ye gone soft writin' stories?" a large man asked from behind a roped-off area that contained logs the length of three men.

"Who's asking?" Shawn replied, a frown crossing his face.

"I am. Show off for the pretty lady on yer arm, lad, or are ye too much of a coward to do so?"

"Do you mind if I go off for a time to log throw?" Shawn folded up his sleeves and pulled the tails of his shirt out of his pants as he spoke.

Brianna shook her head and watched him duck under the rope to converse with a group of men already behind the ropes. He slapped the man beside him and threw back his head and laughed at something he said. Brianna had never seen him so – happy.

Right before he picked up a huge log, he glanced her way and winked. At first, she turned to look behind her, then realized the wink was meant for her and flushed with embarrassment.

She was mesmerized by the play of muscles in his arms when he lifted the enormous log onto his shoulder, then sent it sailing through the air. She watched it land on the ground, much farther away from the other logs that scattered the area. The crowd of people around her roared with applause.

Her chin tilted up with swelling pride for her husband, temporary or not. When he glanced her way this time, she made sure to smile and wave back at him.

After two more throws, he walked over to her.

"Shawn, ye never lose yer touch, do ye, lad?" an elderly man shouted from the crowd.

"Especially not with the ladies," the man beside her added, making Brianna uncomfortable with the way his eyes traveled the length of her.

"'Tis me wife. Mrs. Fraser, meet Jacob Fraser," Shawn introduced.

"Wife! I never thought I'd see the day!" the elderly man stated, pushing his way through the crowd toward Brianna.

"Are you a relation of my husband's?" Brianna asked.

Shawn spoke before the old man had a chance. "We think the lines of our families crossed back in Scotland. Probably a very distant cousin of some sort, but clan no less," Shawn stated firmly with a friendly slap to the man's back.

Old Jacob Fraser took Brianna's hand in his aged one and said, "'Tis good to see the lad has settled down with such a beautiful woman. I can die knowing that the Fraser name will continue on thanks to ye, lass."

Shawn's face split into a huge grin. She wanted to kick him for his dishonesty. Instead, she pulled her husband aside. "How can you allow this kind old man to assume that our marriage is anything but temporary and that we're going to have children together in the future?"

"Better to let things sit the way they are. No use stirrin' up the pot and causin' people to talk. Word might get back to Charlestown of our special situation and ruin your chances of getting that veil ye're always talkin' about."

"But we're not being truthful."

"Aye, the truth 'tis between God and us. No one else need know. Now, can I have this dance, Mrs. Fraser?"

She slipped her arm through his and asked, "Why do I think you're still keeping something from me?"

He smiled in reply, making her feel even more curious as he guided her onto the dance floor. When she was a little girl, she imagined having children of her own. At least six, she thought, to make a large enough brood to form the family she never had.

"The wheels are turning in yer head, I can nearly see them myself," Shawn commented, dipping his head lower to level with her eyes. "Do ye miss the children at the convent?"

"Yes, I do," she softly replied.

At the start of a new song, many couples joined them dancing, squeezing their bodies uncomfortably close. Her husband seemed determined to talk while swaying to the gentle beat of the music.

"Have ye ever thought about having little babes of yer own?" Shawn whispered in her ear.

She tipped her face up to his, hoping that her deepest desire wasn't written on her face. "You know a nun can never have children of her own."

"I know, lass, but are ye willin' to give that right up?"

Before she had the chance to answer, a member of the band pulled Shawn onto the wooden platform and placed a bagpipe in his hands. At first, he looked unsure of himself, until she watched his fingers slide into place on the instrument.

As soon as he breathed into the mouthpiece, his eyes turned to her and remained throughout the song. The rest of the world melted away, the dancers that jostled her, the conversations going on around her, even the birds singing in the trees. All she saw and heard was her husband playing a tune only for her. The sweet harmony of notes bringing joyful tears to her eyes.

The spell was broken when the elderly Fraser grabbed her hand to dance. Brianna tried to politely refuse, but he insisted, tugging her onto the dance floor before the band of pipers. The way he swung her around made her dizzy with laughter. She would have never imagined a man his age so light on his feet.

When another man was about to take over the dance with her, Shawn appeared by her side. "This lady dances only with her *husband*," he emphasized, his stance reminding her of a warrior. She hid her smile.

He slid his arms around her, pulling her close as their bodies swayed to the music. Leaning her head against his chest, she thought of nothing else but the gentle movement of their hips and the constant drumming of his heart. She would memorize every minute of the ceilidh so that when she lay awake at night in her little bed in the convent, she would remember how special this day had been.

There's no use making a fuss about it, Sister Mary Margaret would say. Brianna heard her words – *stop fretting, child, let God guide your way* – as she sat stiffly on the church pew, careful not to look into the faces of the people around her. She kept her eyes on the simple altar in front of her, hoping that her heart would slow its fearful beat and allow her to breathe easier.

It's not that she didn't want to experience new things. Every day outside of the convent she encountered new places, people, customs of life. This, however, made her stomach feel uneasy. Hadn't she been warned against this faith? Weren't all the people sitting beside her lost souls from the one true religion?

"Relax, Bri, a Protestant church 'tis a church like any other. Ye look like ye're waitin' for them to slip a noose around yer neck," Shawn whispered into her ear.

She nodded woodenly without actually turning her head. No vessels holding holy water, an empty cross, no saints' pictures on the walls, and he expected her to stay calm?

He leaned in close, making her heart beat even more erratically. "New experiences, remember, lass. Keep yer eyes on the black veil."

"What?" she asked softly out of the corner of her mouth.

"The black veil ye've coveted since ye were a young lass," he added as if she had gone daft.

"Right, the black veil," she replied, just now realizing it was the first time she thought about the veil in days. She hated to admit that with each new day in Halifax, the ache of longing to return to the convent became a little less.

She found that she had already grown accustomed to the lack of ringing bells and would find herself in conversation with God at all times of day, without the constraint of bells telling her to pray.

When the chords of the organist vibrated the walls of the church, Brianna leaned forward to grab a hymnal from the shelf in front of her. *New experiences*, she repeated to herself. *Remember the black veil.*

When she opened the book and flipped through the pages, she found no musical notes, only words. Her hand covered her gasp when she turned over the cover of the small black book and read the words *Holy Bible.*

"'Tis only the Bible, lass. It won't bite," Shawn joked, noticing the shocked expression on her face.

"But why isn't it on the altar for the priest to read?" she whispered, holding the book reverently in her hands.

"We've no priests, only pastors in the Protestant church. There are a few Bibles in each pew to read along when the pastor reads scripture. Haven't ye ever flipped through one before?"

She shook her head and placed the book back on the shelf from which she took it, not comfortable with the idea of reading the words of such a holy book.

"Greetings, fellow brothers and sisters in Christ!" The pastor wore a wide smile standing at the pulpit. "Special congratulations to one of our own, Shawn Fraser, who recently married Miss Brianna Lawrence from Charlestown, Massachusetts."

Shawn stood at the sound of applause, pulling Brianna up with him. The fact that they were in church deceiving all these good people made her feel miserable. She forced a smile on her flush face, hating to be dishonest when she looked at all the familiar faces from the ceilidh sending their warm smiles of congratulations.

Aunt Liddea leaned over to Shawn and Brianna when they sat back down. "I forgot to mention that I spoke to Pastor McOliver this morning and told him about your marriage."

"Aye, did ye forget to mention anything else?" Shawn asked.

An elderly woman patted Brianna's hand. "He's lucky to have you, dear."

Brianna had to admit that the well wishes of the people around her calmed her racing heart. How many times had she been warned about this church growing up in the convent? Just sitting in a church that wasn't Catholic was supposed to be sacrilegious, but it didn't feel that way to her. It felt different, but not different in a bad way.

When the pastor read scripture, her curious eyes slanted over to Shawn's Bible. He nudged the book toward her, pointing to the passage the pastor was reading. She leaned in closer to him and followed along, her whole body tingling with excitement. Holy Scripture felt personal, more intimate, when she read the words to herself. She couldn't wait to tell the nuns back home.

Music began shortly after scripture, the songs of worship breathing new life into her faith. Shawn's baritone voice blended beautifully with the congregation of singers, moving her to sing alongside him.

At first, she sang softly, mouthing the words as she did in the convent, her voice little more than a whisper. As voices rose in unison beside her, it encouraged her to lift her own voice high in song like never before. It felt freeing, exhilarating, to sing out her faith. She held nothing back, the melody bursting forth from her lips, lightening her heart. The string of notes sailing her away to a place that stirred more than her heart and dug deep into her soul.

With the last note sung, her mood plummeted until she opened her eyes to the sound of applause. Embarrassed, she found herself standing alone and quickly sat back down on the pew.

"Ye've got the voice of an angel," Shawn stated. "Where have ye been hidin' that?"

"Hiding it?" Brianna asked, confused.

"I never heard such a beautiful voice. Did ye sing at the convent?"

"Reverend Mother always reminded me to lower my voice since I wasn't a choir nun," she whispered.

"'Tis a crime to harbor such a voice. That sweet sound was meant for all to hear," Shawn stated, "and not jus I feel that way, Bri. Look around ye, they've never heard the voice of an angel before now."

At the sound of a gunshot echoing against the church walls, Shawn covered Brianna's body and pushed her down to the floor. It all happened so quickly, she didn't know what to think. One minute she was sinfully basking in the praise Shawn was showering on her, and the next her body was being squished between the pew and the floor.

Aunt Liddea tugged Shawn up with a laugh. "A bit jumpy, aren't ye? The little lad up front jumped off of his seat onto the floor."

Shawn helped Brianna up onto the pew and looked around him embarrassed. "I thought the noise was a gunshot," he admitted sheepishly.

He straightened her hat on her head and pushed back wayward strands of hair that had slipped out of her braid. "Are ye all right?"

At her nod, he breathed a sigh of relief and tried to relax.

The danger that Brianna was in in Charlestown still lingered at the corners of his mind. Even here, she was a Catholic in a community of Protestants. Would her life always be in jeopardy because of her religion? He knew he was reacting first, thinking later, which was foolish, since he knew the people in this town meant no harm to her. Of course, no one actually knew she was Catholic either.

At the end of the service, Pastor McOliver shook her hand

exuberantly. "I had to personally meet you, Mrs. Fraser, and invite you to sing at our humble church anytime. It was pure pleasure to my ears."

Shawn received the telegraph as soon as they arrived back at his aunts' cottage.

Riot soon. Stop. Your story to print. Stop. Come back or lose payment. Stop.

Brianna stood at the threshold of their bedroom, watching Shawn throw clothes into his bag.

"You're leaving?" she asked, her voice soft with shock.

He rubbed her arms up and down, needing to feel her warmth one last time before he left. "I've unfinished business to deal with in Charlestown."

"I'll come with you." When he was about to shake his head, she quickly added, "I won't be any trouble." She heard the pleading in her own voice but couldn't help the fear she felt at the idea of being alone.

"Safer for ye here, Bri. I'll come back soon enough and we'll talk more," he stated.

"Safer, what do you mean by safer? What's happening in Charlestown?"

"This has nothin' to do with ye. Ye're to trust me here. I'll be back soon enough."

He swept her into his arms and kissed her soundly, thoroughly, taking her breath away, her mind so clouded from his kiss that it took several minutes before she realized he had already grabbed his bag and walked out of the room.

By the time she hurried down the stairs and looked out the front door, he had saddled up his horse and was riding down the road toward town.

"I can't believe he's going without me," Brianna voiced softly, tears balancing on the rims of her eyes.

"He'll be back," Aunt Liddea assured from behind her.

Aunt Bea put her arm around Brianna's shoulder. "There must

have been something mighty important in that telegram for him to leave ye so soon, dear."

"He really did leave me," Brianna mumbled.

"We know that boy loves ye whether he's ready to admit it or not. He'll be back," Aunt Liddea declared.

Brianna sat down on the chair and stared out the window toward the road. "He doesn't love me. I'm only a temporary inconvenience in his life. He felt he owed me for the care I gave him in the convent so he brought me to Halifax on this extended vacation. At the end of the month, he plans to bring me back to the convent and have the marriage annulled. Please, don't think I'm ungrateful, because I have enjoyed the holiday immensely." She bit down hard on her lip, fighting to hold in the tears that threatened to fall.

"It's time I told you a little story, dear," Aunt Liddea began, patting Brianna's hands. "Shawn's mother was a deeply religious woman. She even went to live in a convent for a short spell to be schooled, but instead the young, impressionable girl fell in love with a young priest."

Brianna's hand flew to her mouth in shock.

Aunt Liddea continued. "She wrote to my sister and me often, we being the only relatives she had left. I knew her heart would be broken and pleaded with her to leave the convent before the entanglement deepened. She explained that she loved him too much to leave him. Soon our deepest fears came true. She became pregnant with his child. The priest, we assumed, feared to lose his position at the church and so denied that the child was his and broke the poor gil's heart. The senior priest sent her back to us as soon as he heard of the situation.

"Her nights back home with us were filled with nightmares. During the day, she walked through the house with dark circles under her eyes and hardly an expression on her face. Only a few days after she gave birth to Shawn, she took her own life. Sister and I assumed that she couldn't live with a broken heart."

Aunt Liddea squeezed Brianna's shoulder.

"Go on, sister, finish the story," Aunt Bea urged.

"We raised Shawn from that day forward. Thank goodness there was the two of us. He was quite a handful at times. Full of questions, he was, especially concerning his mother. When he reached an age where we thought he could begin to understand the matter, we explained things to him. He needed to be told the truth in order to be fair to his dear mother's memory.

"Once he grew into a man, he went off in search of the details that we couldn't give him about his parentage. His nose for details made him into the reporter he is today. We're so proud of what he accomplished in his life.

"The only thing that worries us is the deep hatred he carries inside his heart toward the Catholic Church. It began the day we told him the story of his mother and seemed to grow over the years to eventually consume his daily life. His snide comments about Catholics in his letters home to us or on visits here began to worry us."

"I can't believe he married me. I'm Catholic," Brianna stated, confused.

"That's why we know he loves you, dear. He never would have married a Catholic if he didn't love you." Aunt Bea turned to her sister. "Would he, sister?"

"No, he wouldn't," Aunt Liddea replied with a firm nod.

"Before he married me, he told me he had a debt to pay in my regard and a need for a wife in name only. He said marriage would end the constant badgering of mothers shoving their eligible daughters his way," Brianna explained.

Aunt Bea took both of Brianna's hands in hers and looked directly into her eyes. "Shawn would never take the holy bonds of matrimony so lightly as to go into it to pay off a debt. I could never believe that of him. As for the mothers badgering him, making him marry – that's just sheer nonsense." She turned to Aunt Liddea. "Isn't that so, sister?" Aunt Liddea nodded, a smile forming on her face.

Aunt Bea turned to Aunt Liddea. "Are you thinking what I'm thinking?"

Both aunts stood up. "Brianna, grab your hat, dear! We're riding into town!"

Brianna began to twist her hands together on her lap. "Shawn will be upset with me if he thinks I'm chasing after him. Do you think he'll still be there?" Brianna snatched up her hat and pinned it in place on her head.

"Don't worry about Shawn, dear. We'll handle him. The two of you shouldn't be separated so soon after your nuptials. I'm sure Captain McAndry will agree with us there. The boy never knew what was good for him," Aunt Liddea mumbled as she hurried out the back door towards the barn.

The waves splashed over the side of the ship, lapping water onto the deck as thunder rolled overhead. With each pitch of the ship, Brianna's arms wrapped tightly around the post, praying not to be thrown into the ocean by the forceful winds of the storm.

Captain McAndry stowed her away on ship without Shawn being aware. It had been a long two days hidden in a tiny cabin with only the captain knowing her whereabouts. She had fallen asleep that night with dreams of telling Shawn in the morning that she followed him on board ship. The captain advised her to wait two days so that the ship would be too far down the coast to sail back.

Instead of sleep, she awoke on deck in the middle of a storm, fighting for her life. Her sleepwalking was getting out of control.

One minute she was sleeping and the next she was scrambling to grab hold of anything to keep her body from sliding off deck. A huge wave slammed against the side of the ship. Rain slashed her skin while lightning cracked overhead. The sea tirelessly lapped water over her, wrenching her body away from the pole she fought to hold.

"Bri, what the hell are ye doin' here?"

At the sound of his voice, she silently thanked God. Until she looked up into his angry eyes. At the sudden tilt of the ship, his large arms wrapped around her and the pole, keeping her from losing her grip.

"Answer me! What are ye doin' here?" he bellowed above the sound of the rain pelting the deck and the wind howling above them.

"I wanted to be with you!" she shouted back.

"Great, now, we can die together!" He struggled to keep hold of the pole as the ship dipped into the sea.

"I have faith in you!" Brianna yelled into his ear, sending shivers down his spine.

His arms hugged her tighter against him.

He had endured many storms upon these seas, but never one as violent as this one. Between the drenching cold rain, wave upon wave slashed against the deck of the ship threatening to pull their bodies apart. He kept awake throughout the night, vowing to keep his wife alive until the morning.

The storm let up just as the first rays of the morning sun burst through the clouds. When Brianna's eyes fluttered open, she found herself safely tucked within his arms.

He looked down at her face still clouded with sleep and exhaled a breath he didn't know he held. His wife risked her life *just to be with him*. He braced himself against the warm feeling, remembering that he promised Brianna that the marriage would be in name only. She would be free to do whatever she pleased once the month of August passed and he felt she was not in any harm. It would be unfair to Brianna if he took advantage of her during that time as much as every cell in his body craved to make her his own for all time. He watched the clouds clear from her green eyes as they focused on him.

She snuggled closer against him. "Is the storm over?"

He rested his forehead on hers. "Aye, we made it through. Now, what should I do with ye? Whatever made ye risk yer life to be with the likes of me?"

When she didn't answer, he added, "How did ye make it into town before the ship set sail and board without my knowledge?"

"Well," she hedged, "Aunt Liddea and Aunt Bea had errands to tend to in town, so I rode along," she explained, not wanting Shawn to be upset with his aunts.

"And did ye tiptoe on board?" he began, then hesitated. "McAndry had a hand in this, too, didn't he? Me aunts made certain ye accomplished the task, but why?"

She was too honest not to give him the truth. "They felt that since we were only recently married, we shouldn't be apart. Please don't be mad at them! They all love you so much!"

"And ye, Brianna, what do ye think of me?" Shawn asked, his lips a whisper away from her mouth.

"You're my husband and I want to stay with you – until the

month is up," she quickly added. "I was going to tell you I was here, but the captain suggested I wait until the second day of the voyage so that you couldn't force the ship to turn around to go back to Halifax." Brianna covered her mouth with her hand after she finished her rambling.

His finger came up to gently lift a tendril of wet hair from her face. She leaned her cheek against his hand. "I *was* going to come back."

The green of her eyes deepened. "You were?"

"Aye, how can a man stand to be away from a wife as beautiful as ye, lass, even temporarily?" His lips touched hers lightly, smoothly, just enough to ease the ache that pulsed through his body.

Captain McAndry cleared his throat behind them. "I see the two of ye survived the mighty storm."

Shawn cleared his throat. His passion changed to anger. "No thanks to ye. Me wife wouldn't have been in any danger if ye didn't give in to the aunts."

"What can I say? They're a persuasive lot, the two of them, promising me this pie and that when I arrived back in a week or two," Captain McAndry stated with a smile, his hands raised and dropped to his side. "I suggest ye stop yer whining and take yer wife down to yer cabin to change before she becomes ill."

Shawn turned to look at Brianna's shivering wet form. "He's right, I wouldn't want ye to get sick after survivin' such a storm."

He hurried down the stairs with Brianna tucked safely against him. Fevers struck quickly and were difficult to control.

Before entering the cabin, she confessed, "I left in such a rush that I didn't bring anything with me, not even extra clothes."

"Ye can wear a shirt of mine until yer clothes dry. Come in and let me help ye out of those wet things."

He tried to think of anything besides the fact that he was unbuttoning his wife's gown – temporary wife's gown – *his wife in name only*, he reminded himself. After unfastening only the first couple of buttons, his fingers shook so much that he gave up. Instead, he pulled out a shirt from his trunk and strode to the door of the cabin.

"Try this shirt on for size. I'll go and see if I can brew ye a cup of tea," he stated. He breathed easy as soon as the door shut firmly behind him.

Brianna slid out of her wet dress and petticoat and hung them on hooks on the wall. Then she slipped on Shawn's thick cotton shirt, enjoying the soft feel of it against her skin. Her hands moved over the smooth material, her fingers lightly rubbing up and down her arms.

Shawn nearly dropped the cup of tea he was carrying when he walked back into the room. His eyes tried not to glance at her standing tall, only his thin shirt to conceal the feminine curves of her petite frame.

He shook his head, fighting the emotions that fought to be released. His brow damp with sweat, he stepped toward her, using every ounce of willpower he possessed. He fought not to give in to his deepest desires and make her his permanently.

"The cook gave me a cup of broth to warm yer bones," he muttered.

Mesmerized, he watched her sit down on the bed. The edge of his shirt rode up her leg, exposing the shape of her calf all the way up to her knee. Quickly, he strode over, with shaky hands placed the broth on the bedside table, and shoved her body under the covers of the bed.

After he tucked her up to her chin in blankets, he sighed with relief. Now, if only he could keep her that way for the entire month of August.

CHAPTER NINE

Charlestown seemed quiet, much too quiet for the early hours of dusk.

The door of the boarding house swung open as Shawn approached. A middle-aged woman, thin, with dark black hair twisted up on her head, stood in the open doorway. She wore a mildly curious expression on her face.

"So she's the one," she stated to Shawn.

"Mrs. Benson, allow me to introduce my wife," Shawn stated.

"So ya married her, too, did ya now?" his landlady asked.

"Yer losin' me, Mrs. Benson," Shawn replied.

"Come in, come in. Once the town gets wind that you're back with the girl, they'll be knockin' on your door," Mrs. Benson stated, opening the door wider.

Shawn ushered her into the house. Then turned his attention back to Mrs. Benson.

"Ye've really lost me here, Mrs. Benson. Please be startin' at the beginnin'."

"It's all over town that another girl from the convent on the hill has escaped over the fence. They searched through town with a sketch of her face, searching for her. She's the girl, isn't she?" She looked pointedly at her. Brianna stood still under her gaze, too shocked to say a word.

"'Tis the lass from the convent, but she didn't escape, I *married* her," he explained.

"Married, ya say! Some would say 'tis one and the same. Either way, she escaped the clutches of the church and all the evil that occurs on that hill," Mrs. Benson stated with disdain.

"I've to show my new wife to my apartment, if ye don't mind," he replied, brushing past Mrs. Benson.

"Shawn, what's goin' on? Why do they think such things?" Brianna asked.

He waited until he entered his set of rooms in the house to answer. The door opened to one large bedroom with a small dressing room set off to the left side.

"I don't know, Bri, but I'll straighten it all out. Rumors are nasty things and get out of hand fairly quickly, but I've an inklin' as to who might have begun this one."

He started for the door, hesitated, and turned to take the two steps that would place his large frame directly in front of her. His arms lifted her petite frame to his height while his lips sought hers. It was a soft, sweet kiss, gently taken and gently received, making it all the harder for him to leave.

"Tonight, I've things to explain to ye," he said softly in promise.

He slammed the door at the newspaper office with such force it nearly shook the entire building, causing everyone to stop and step away as he strode into his boss's office. Once there, he walked inside and slammed the door shut behind him.

"Back so soon? Trouble with your new wife?" his boss calmly asked with a slight grin on his face, his squinty black eyes studying him.

"How did ye find out I married the gil?" Shawn demanded.

"Well, well, well ... so you *did* run off and marry the nun! I wasn't certain until just now."

"What have you done? I've given ye no story to print."

"Done? I've done nothing but set up your story line for you. This is an opportunity of a lifetime! It'll sell newspapers across the state, hell, even the country! Here, read this, I've even outlined it all, thinking your head might still be too clouded with your new wife," he said with a sneer.

Shawn read the first couple of lines, then crumbled the paper into his hand.

"This is never goin' to run! I told ye I found no story to tell at that convent. Now, ye think to fabricate stories about me wife!" he exclaimed. "Ye're nothin' but a greed-infested shyster that allows his hate to cloud the truth of a story."

"Don't forget that you came looking for a job at the *Protestant* with that same hate tucked inside you. You're no different than I am," Snead stated with contempt.

"That's where ye're wrong. I report only the true facts of the story and have enough integrity not to allow greed or hate to persuade me," Shawn replied, controlling the impulse to smash his fist into Snead's face.

"There's going to be a story either way, with or without your so-called wife. The story of the last nun that jumped the fence has already riled the town's people. When your wife's story prints, the people in this town will finally get rid of that devil's den of nuns."

Shawn's fist pounded on the desk in front of him. "I'll have no part of this. And if ye think to run any story about me wife, it'll be the last story ye ever publish!"

"I don't take kindly to threats, Fraser, especially since ye still work here!" his boss replied, his face red with anger.

"Not anymore," Shawn stated and walked out of his office and out of the building. There were other newspapers all over this country, ones that reported the *real* news not fabricated stories.

Shawn stormed back into the boarding house full of anger. He told himself that he should be out searching for another job now that he had a wife to support – for the month of August at least. Instead, his feet led him right back to his wife.

When he ripped open the door to his rooms, his eyes went wide as his jaw dropped to the floor. Lying in a huge tub of steaming hot water in the middle of his room was his wife – stark naked.

"Shawn!" Brianna screeched. Her hands grabbed for the towel beside the tub.

He opened his mouth to speak, but no sound came out.

"What are you doing here? You said you wouldn't be back until later today!" she explained.

He was her husband, damn it, and had every right to be here. Shawn took two steps toward his wife and watched her eyes widen, gripping the towel to her body like a shield. He watched her face turn scarlet red with embarrassment, and for some reason that bothered him – a lot.

He was sick and tired of doing the right thing all of the time. His hands dipped into the tub and scooped his clean, chaste, wet wife out of the water and onto the bed. She scrambled under the covers, soaking wet, the towel wrapped tightly around her.

He followed her onto the bed and sat on the edge of it, pulling off his boots, one at a time, allowing them to drop heavily onto the floor with a thud. Next his socks, and lastly he pulled the hem of his shirt over his head.

At the sound of her gasp, he turned to see his precious wife faint back onto the pillow of the bed. *Just like old times*, he thought with a grim chuckle, which only made him realize that he was allowing his anger to control his actions. Brianna deserved so much more than that. Gently, he shook her awake.

"Ye're no goin' to faint again, are ye?" He smiled down at her when she shook her head slowly against his shoulder. His hand gently lifted her chin to face him.

"I promised I'd not take the liberties of a normal husband so that our marriage remained on paper only, but now I feel a need to discuss that option with ye," he began.

Since she made no comment, holding the quilt of the bed firmly beneath her chin, he continued. "I've feelings for ye, lass, that confuse me more than I can say. I wanted to keep this marriage on paper only incase ye wished to return to the convent. Without the union of a man and woman, the marriage can be annulled at the end of the month."

"Are you saying you want to leave me again?" she asked softly into the quiet of the room.

"Quite the opposite. I'm saying I don't ever want ye to leave. I've grown to care for ye, but I'm no too certain how ye feel on the matter."

A loud knock startled their conversation. "Convenient timing for an interruption, isn't it now?" he remarked, irritated.

He opened the door, and his landlady handed him a note. "Messenger dropped this off for you."

He read the note, grabbed for his clothes, and dressed quickly. "I've got to go, but I'll be back later tonight. Promise me ye'll stay safely in this house and not follow me out tonight." He waited until she slowly nodded before he left the room.

Hot didn't begin to describe how he felt, standing in the room crowded with spectators, listening to Lyman Beecher's speech on the corruption of the Roman Catholic Church, especially when he had a beautiful wife waiting for him in his bed. His informant told him it was the last of three speeches the man would make in the Boston area.

His words created a frenzy of excitement that seemed to ripple across the crowds of men. He spoke of the growing numbers of Catholics in the country increasing over Protestants. Anti-democratic he called the whole lot of them, to which a roar of applause sounded. He specifically warned of Catholic schools catering to educate "our Protestant children."

"I don't hear you cheering," Snead remarked out of the corner of his mouth, sidling up next to him. The arrogant presence of the man made him want to place his hands around his throat and squeeze tight.

"I should have known ye'd be here," Shawn replied with barely a glance.

"Don't take the high road with me. You're standing in the same room for all the same reasons."

"I'm here out of curiosity, nothing else. If I had known slime like ye would be crawling out from under their rocks, I would have stayed home," Shawn stated with disgust. He ignored his ex-boss and turned his attention back to the speaker.

Snead shrugged off his comment. "Think what you like. It's people like me that are going to save this country's democratic way of life. After tonight's speech, there won't be a need for a story from you. These men are ready to take action to save the basic principles that this fine land was founded on."

"By frightening defenseless women in a monastery?" Shawn asked.

"You've gone soft now that you have a Catholic wife," Snead sneered, puffing the smoke of his cigar in Shawn's direction.

Shawn brushed his comment off and turned to leave the room. "Soft? I think I've finally come to my senses."

Disgusted, he strode outside away from the lecture hall. The last person he wanted to see walked up to him. His father had a way of irritating him just with his presence.

"What are you doing back? Where's Brianna? Is she all right?"

"I had business in town," Shawn stated and began to walk away. His father grabbed hold of his arm to stop him.

Shawn looked down at the hand that held him, then back at his father. "My wife is fine. Is there something else ye want?"

His father dropped his hand. "Did you hear enough of Beecher?"

"Depends on what ye mean by enough," Shawn remarked.

His father rubbed his lower lip with his hand. Shawn had just lifted his hand to do the same but quickly lowered it. "Brianna is well, then?"

"I've already stated that fact. She's restin' at home."

An uncomfortable silence ensued.

"Any news in there," his father asked, tilting his head towards the lecture hall, "about a riot at the convent?"

"If I was to guess, I'd say within a day or so something is goin' to happen. I'm jus not sure what," Shawn ventured. "I'd warn the Reverend Mother if I were ye."

He arrived back at the boarding house late that night and left early the next morning, assuring her heavy, sleep-filled eyes that he would be back by nightfall. When she opened her mouth to object, he brushed aside her questions with a soul-searching kiss. He left a few minutes later, her mind so muddled that she couldn't remember what she was going to ask him.

The first thing she thought of when she awoke was the last thing she thought of before falling asleep – *he really, truly cared for her. He wanted to stay with her forever.* No one had ever cared about her like that. Her father might have cared about her when she was a little girl, but she couldn't remember that far back. She couldn't wait until nightfall to be in Shawn's arms again.

Humming her way through the day, she tried to make herself useful while waiting for him to come home. She cleaned every inch of the little set of rooms until the floors and walls shone brightly.

The hours of the day ticked by slowly. She sat and ate lunch with Mrs. Benson, but the woman's nosiness irritated her. She felt that Mrs. Benson befriended her only for the facts that she could give her about the convent.

Back in her rooms, Brianna said a quick prayer of forgiveness for her unkind thoughts toward Mrs. Benson and promised to try to be more understanding toward the woman tomorrow.

Finally, she decided she'd wash some clothes to make the long afternoon hours pass by. She emptied out the pockets of Shawn's clothing and found a folded sheet of paper tucked deep inside his vest pocket. Her first impulse was to put it back, but her curious side carefully unfolded the paper and smoothed it out on the desk nearby. There was a need in her to find out everything about her new husband, especially what he wrote in his newspaper articles.

Tears slipped down her cheeks onto the crinkled paper as she read the words written upon its surface. Words she gave him in confidence that he twisted for his own use. Her heart wrenched with pain, thinking of the depth of his betrayal for the sake of a story.

She sat down on the edge of the bed, her head spinning, her stomach twisted into tight knots of despair, and tried to make sense of it all. Did she really mean so little to him? Was everything a lie, after all they shared?

The more she thought about his betrayal, the more her anguish turned to anger. He had turned around every word she confided to him about the Reverend Mother to use for his own selfish reasons at the newspaper. Word for word the shameful story of Mother's overindulgence spread across the page, neatly written in her husband's script.

A chill ran down her spine when she noticed the treasured song sheet she thought she had lost at the convent, sitting behind his story. The only possession she had of her mother stolen by her own husband.

She crossed her arms tightly around herself, rocking back and forth on the edge of the bed, her chest tightening uncomfortably with the extent of her husband's deception. Tears ran freely down her face, blinding her.

Once every tear had been shed, she slowly got up from the bed and splashed cold water on her face. God would be her only comfort now. She went in search of His presence.

Shawn stomped into the boarding house, tired and dirt-encrusted. He found out that the riot was planned for tonight and that the men were all to congregate outside of the convent gates at dusk.

He hurried toward the back of the house and Brianna.

"She's not there," his landlady called out to him, stopping him in his steps. "I checked earlier."

"What do you mean she's not here? Did ye not see her leave?"

"I had lunch with your missus near to noon, then she went off to your rooms to do laundry. I haven't seen her since. Probably slipped out the back door to do errands and such. Ya know how the young ladies are."

He went back into his set of rooms and paced back and forth along the floor, impatiently waiting for her. His eyes scanned the room for a clue as to her whereabouts, then spotted the sheet of paper flattened on his desk. His traitorous words smudged by her tears.

He knew that she'd run to the convent for comfort. He only hoped that he could find her before the riot began.

CHAPTER TEN

Brianna held in the flood of tears threatening to fall, her body trembling with emotion. She knocked on the large wooden door of the convent. When no answer came, she became more insistent, knocking louder, desperate for entrance. She was about to run to the side door of the building when the door swung open with such force that she stepped back startled.

Mother stood stoically in the open doorway, wearing a sour expression on her solemn face. It softened the instant she recognized Brianna.

She poked her head out, searching into the shadows of dusk.

"Brianna, why aren't you in Halifax, and where is Mr. Fraser?"

"I need to talk to you, Mother," Brianna stated quietly, blinking back tears, her voice raw with emotion.

Mother's face became flustered, her eyes searching into the growing darkness. "Now is not the time, Brianna. I've important matters to deal with tonight. Those miscreants from town are on their way and are threatening to burn down the convent."

"I desperately need your advice," Brianna pleaded, wringing her hands.

"Pray for the answers you need, Brianna," her Superior instructed, turning away distractedly.

"I...." Brianna began, but her Superior left her side to stand in the open doorway, arms crossed tightly in front of her.

Quickly, she made her way to the chapel, frantic for the solace only God could give her. There, she knelt and began the prayers that flowed from her heart, finding comfort with the familiarity of each recitation.

She blocked out the muffled shouts from outside and frantically tried to concentrate on the words of her prayers. Her mind kept wandering off to the last conversation with her husband. *I care for you, he said, or rather, he cared for the information she was blindly supplying him,* she thought angrily. Her hands squeezed tightly together against the raw pain of his betrayal while her lips pleaded with God for answers.

She failed at everything she attempted to do as a nun and now as a wife. What was she to do? She felt like a piece of property purchased for the sake of a story. She knew nothing of the man she called husband except for the fact that he was a liar. With the back of her hand, she wiped away the tears that stained her face, bowed her head, and allowed the peace which only came with prayer to transcend upon her.

Shawn steered his horse through the mobs of people gathering around the gates of the convent. Bottles of whiskey passed among the crowd between angry shouts of slurs against the Superior of the nunnery.

He spotted the Reverend Mother standing on the threshold of the front door, her formidable form looking down at the angry crowd with disdain.

"Leave the premises immediately, or I'll get every Irishman in this town and the next to burn down your houses and places of business!" she warned.

In response, the already enraged men shook their fists into the air. Shawn knew the Reverend Mother's threatening words only incited the men's anger further.

They demanded to see the nun that ran away. The Reverend Mother shook her head and waved away their threats. The sound of two gunshots urged him into action.

He shoved his way through the crowd of rebel rousers, some of which wore face paint like Indians, and slipped through the gate unnoticed onto the convent grounds. There, he crept up the drive, careful to stay in shadow as he hurried his way up the hill to the main building of the convent, and burst open the kitchen door.

All eyes turned to him when he stepped inside. "Does anyone know where Brianna is?"

Sister Mary Clarence looked up startled. "Mr. Fraser, she's not here. Isn't she supposed to be with you?" Then she quietly added, for his ears only, "There's men outside threatening us. We need to get the children out."

The nuns stood in the center of the kitchen, gathering the children into a group, calling out names. A light tug on his hand made him glance down to see two big brown eyes looking up at him. He recognized the little wide-eyed lass from his walk in the gardens a few weeks back.

"I'm scared. Are those bad men coming in here to hurt us?" she asked, melting his heart.

He bent his knees to level his eyes with hers. "I won't allow anyone to harm ye, little one." He picked her up and held her tightly in his arms.

"Ye all must be very brave and very quiet," he warned the group of children and nuns. To Sister Mary Clarence, he said, "I'll take ye through the opening in the fence behind the gardens, from there ye can walk to the neighbor's house for refuge."

"Thank you, Mr. Fraser. I appreciate your help. I'm afraid I'm a bit overwhelmed," Sister Mary Clarence replied.

"Given the circumstances, ye've a right to be. All right now, everyone form a line behind me," he directed, holding his finger to his lips to hush the group before starting out.

Quietly, Shawn led the band of children and nuns out of the building, careful to stay in the shadows of trees to prevent being seen. With the yelling that came from the rambunctious crowd, Shawn feared that these men were riled up and capable of doing anything, including harming these young girls.

He breathed a sigh of relief once they reached the gardens without incident and slipped through the opening in the fence.

Once the entire group made it through, he pulled Sister Mary Clarence aside and said, "Ye walk straight through the fields here a short way to safety, Sister. I'm goin' back inside."

The frightened nun grasped hold of his hand. "God be with you, sir."

"Thank ye, Sister," Shawn replied.

He hurried back to the area, noticing that the men had edged their way closer to the building, gathering around the convent's grounds. Several threw torches through the windows, laughing and rejoicing as the window dressings burst into flames.

Shawn knew he had a limited amount of time to search the building before it was engulfed in flames. He quickly slipped back inside amid the dense smoke and felt his way along the halls, shouting out Brianna's name.

Outside the chapel's door, he hesitated. He thought he heard a woman's voice but wasn't quite sure. The minute he entered the chapel, he sighed with relief. Brianna sat in a pew, her head bowed low in prayer.

"Brianna, I've found ye, lass!" Shawn exclaimed, rushing down the aisle toward her, his heart in his throat.

"I'm talking to God, go away!" she replied, angry tears streaming down her cheeks.

His eyes glanced back at the entrance to the chapel. "There's no time to talk. They'll be here any minute, let's go!"

She stubbornly sat in her pew, her back ramrod straight. "*Who* are you talking about?"

"The angry mob outside, lass. Let's go!" Shawn urged, his level of patience thinning.

"No harm will come to me in the house of the Lord," she calmly replied, folding her hands primly on her lap, which only frustrated him more.

"Those Protestants mean to burn the whole place down, chapel and all!" he stated loudly, pulling her from her seat against her will.

"But *you're* Protestant," she began and pushed his hands away.

"Bri, there's no time to explain. We have to get out of here! 'Tis a matter of life or death!" He scooped her small frame into his arms.

Brianna fought his hold, pounding her fists against his chest. "Leave me alone. I'm happy here! At least they don't *lie* to me!" she shrieked.

He looked down at her, his eyebrow raised high. "I promise I'll explain everything as soon as I get ye safely out of here. Jus stop yer struggling or we'll both be trapped inside."

"I'm to believe a promise given by a known liar, a Protestant no less!"

"We share the same faith in God. It doesn't matter the buildin' we worship in." The words slid easily off his tongue, surprising even him.

"I know for a fact that you hate Catholics, so what's the real reason you're here, *husband*?"

"Yer me wife," he said simply and continued down the aisle toward the altar with her in his arms.

"Stop." Brianna grabbed the ciborium off the altar. "Mother would want me to save this." She hid the vessel in her arms and covered her mouth with her sleeve when thick smoke filled the chapel from the open door.

Shawn ran out of the back of the building through the gardens to the small mausoleum where the nuns and priests were buried. It contained a small chapel in the back. He tucked her body behind it.

Church bells rang in the distance, alerting the fire companies.

"Wait here," he ordered, not wanting to leave her for even a minute but needing to make certain the voice he heard earlier was not a woman trapped inside the building. "I have to make sure everyone is safely off the grounds."

Brianna stood still in the corner of the small dark building, her thoughts swaying back to her husband's words. He never did give her the real reason why he was here on the same night that these hoodlums were massacring the convent grounds. Maybe he was here to do the same thing. She knew how much he hated all Catholics. The more she thought on the matter, the more fear she felt waiting for him to return. She was just about to leave her hiding place and make her own way to safety when the sound of footsteps nearby made her retreat back into the dark corner.

Her eyes, wide with fear, watched the only home she knew go up in flames. The sounds of crowds cheering at the sight made her throat constrict with emotion. *Where are you, Shawn?*

Again, she heard the sound of footsteps running toward the mausoleum. Quickly, she crouched down low, hoping that the blackness of night would keep her hidden.

Brianna held her breath, her heart pounding against her chest as a group of men entered the small mausoleum. Laughing and joking, they stumbled into the small structure. Brianna swallowed her scream, watching the men flip open caskets and drag corpses out, scattering bones across the mausoleum floor.

A small gasp escaped her lips, watching in horror as one man

117

pulled out the teeth of a corpse's skull, laughing hysterically. He pocketed his treasure, then took a swig from the bottle he held in his hand.

Brianna counted four men ransacking the sacred tomb and knew that these were not the only men on the convent grounds. She squeezed her eyes shut and prayed fervently that the slovenly group would leave the small building.

When an overwhelming smell of liquor and sweat filled her nostrils, she opened her eyes and gasped for air.

"Looky here, boys. I found myself a nun!" the drunken man exclaimed.

To her surprise, no one answered the man in front of her and only silence filled the darkness. Her eyes glanced around the small space for the other men but found that she was left alone with the man in front of her.

His arm snaked out and dragged her roughly out of the dark corner. She noticed how his eyes shifted from side to side while she struggled to break free from his hold. He laughed at her useless attempts and guzzled from the bottle he held in his other hand until she heard a sound behind him.

His head snapped around. "Hey, where is everyone?" he mumbled. His eyes searching the darkness.

At another sound, he hit the bottle he held against the side of a casket, leaving the jagged edges exposed. When his arm pulled her tightly against his body, she fought for breath. Fear paralyzed her.

"I'll slit this lady's throat if ye come near me," he threatened the empty darkness.

She had no doubt the man was capable of doing it. The sharp edges of the bottle scraped against the skin of her throat, causing her body to shake uncontrollably.

The man looked nervously into the darkness, twisting around each time he heard a light sound. The flames from the building illuminated the area creating shadows to dance on the walls.

A large figure stepped out of the darkness.

"Let me wife go," Shawn said slowly, stressing each word in a tone of voice that Brianna had never heard before.

The drunken man seemed to relax at the sound of Shawn's voice.

118

"Ye're wrong lad, this is one of those nuns. We need to be rid of the lot of them! The Pope wants to run our America, that's what this is all about! So move away, she's a prize to be dealt with and destroyed!"

The man never saw the fist coming out of the darkness, but Brianna felt the wind of it pass by her as it hit the man smack in the nose. She heard the snap of cartilage as the shocked man stumbled back, dropping the bottle beside him. Shawn took advantage of the man's stunned silence and pushed him to the ground.

His fist pounded his body until Brianna tugged on his shoulder to stop him.

"He had his filthy hands all over ye," Shawn stated quietly.

With disgust, he stared down at his bloodied hands for a second until the sound of the men wreaking havoc on the convent grounds jolted his thoughts. Over his shoulder, he looked back at the flames of the burning buildings and knew that every second they stood here, Brianna's life was in danger.

"Let's get ye out of here, Bri," he announced, guiding her around to the back of the grounds and through an opening in the fence.

They stumbled their way in the dark to the neighbor's house, where he'd directed the nuns and children to seek refuge. Before he knocked on the door, he turned to Brianna with an odd expression on his face. "Ye didn't faint. Even with the culprit ready to slit yer throat, ye didn't flinch."

"I knew you'd save me."

The woman would faint at the drop of his hat, rather shirt, he thought with a grimace, but when facing real danger, she showed more courage than most. His Brianna was full of surprises.

His fist banged loudly on the front door of the home.

The door creaked narrowly open. "What do you want?" the man asked.

"Are the nuns and children here?" Shawn asked.

"Who are you to ask?" the man stated with suspicion.

"They are friends of my wife. We only wish to see that they are safe."

The man opened the door wider and lifted the candle high that he held in his hands, squinting at Brianna. After a moment, he said,

119

"Yes, they're all upstairs. Go on up."

Shawn's heart squeezed with guilt at the scene in front of him. The children and nuns formed a small half circle in front of a large window, their hands linked tightly together. Torn night-dresses, hair in tangles, each figure stood stock-still, staring out the glass window, disbelief in their eyes, watching the flames destroy their beloved home.

Sister Mary Clarence's eyes widened when she spotted Brianna standing quietly at the door of the room. "What are you doing here, child? I thought you were in Nova Scotia."

"We had a change of plans and.... Who would do such a horrible thing?"

There was a catch to Sister Mary Clarence's voice when she answered, "Hatred brings out the worst in a soul. We can only pray that their hearts will turn towards the Lord and the one true religion."

"'Tis thinkin' like that brought on this mess in the first place. There's no such thing as *one true religion*. We all believe in the same God." There, he stated the fact of the matter and felt better for it.

Brianna looked at him strangely, then turned to Sister Mary Clarence. "I don't know how you can be so forgiving, Sister. They're *horrible, horrible* men that are doing this."

Sister Mary Clarence glanced up at him, then placed her arms around Brianna. "It is not for us to judge these men."

Sister Mary Louise crossed the room toward them. "Everything will be all right, Brianna. Mother Superior will make certain of that," she assured.

"Where is Mother?" Brianna's eyes scanned the room for the familiar face of the Reverend Mother.

Sister Mary Clarence's face paled. "She said she would be right behind us when we ushered the children out. Isn't she downstairs?"

Little Jessie began to cry. "What's happened to Reverend Mother?"

"Oh, dear God, if those men have her, she'll be killed," another sister whispered before rapidly doing the sign of the cross with her hand.

"She might be trapped somewhere because of the fire!" Sister Mary John exclaimed, only adding to the growing terror of the little group.

Shawn knelt down in front of Jessie and the other little girls beside her and very calmly pulled out his handkerchief and wiped the tears that fell down their frightened faces. "I know for a fact that the Reverend Mother would want ye to remain calm and not worry about her." His head leaned back and said loudly, "That goes for the lot of ye. No use thinkin' the worst. I'll go back and see if I can find her."

"Please be careful, Shawn, the whole building looks to be in flames," Brianna whispered.

Shawn tapped his finger lightly on her nose. "Make sure ye stay right here, Bri. I don't want to search for ye when I get back."

Dense black smoke hovered over the monastery grounds. He crossed the fields and slipped back through the fence, covering his face with his shirt. He hurried toward the main building, already feeling the heat from the roaring fire in front of him.

Drunken shouts filled the air as Shawn watched the frenzied dance of the angry mob rushing over the land, ripping and shredding everything in their sight. At the sound of glass shattering, he looked up startled. Objects dropped out of the windows above him. He dodged out of the way as harps, guitars, music books, and a piano forte came crashing through the windows of the main building. Sheets of music fluttering through the air, desks, paint boxes, and volumes of books cluttered the ground around him.

When he looked down the hill toward the gates of the convent, thousands of people stood, staring at the flames swallowing up the building. Several engine companies arrived at the scene, but to Shawn's surprise, they stopped at the foot of the hill and sprayed no water at the burning building.

Shawn strained his eyes, searching into the darkness for the Mother Superior, careful to stay out of sight of the other men. He slipped inside the building, worried that the formidable Superior might be stubborn enough to fight until the end to defend her home.

Flames engulfed the kitchen where he entered. He blocked his face with his arms and ran through an opening in the center of the room to the staircase beyond. Coughing and sputtering against the deadly black smoke, he made his way up the stairs, careful of his footing, when the Reverend Mother came crashing into him. She was hurrying down the stairs.

The Reverend Mother's hand flew to her heart. "Mr. Fraser."

He watched in disbelief as the formidable woman straightened her black robe, not perturbed in the least by the events occurring around her.

"I needed to make certain all of my girls were out of the building before leaving. And why are *you* here, Mr. Fraser?"

Shawn arched a disbelieving glance at her. "Don't look at me like that. None of this is my doin'. I warned ye of the danger the convent was in."

He led her down the hall, away from the flames consuming the kitchen. Instead, they searched for a room not heated with flames and ran to the window. Shawn climbed out and checked to make sure no one was near when he helped the Superior in her long bulky robe tumble out of the room's window.

Once the air thinned and they could breathe easily, he angled a look at her. "I'm a little curious as to why ye didn't leave the buildin', knowin' how dangerous it was if they caught sight of ye."

"I already told you, Mr. Fraser. I wanted to make certain the children were all out," she repeated, her voice hoarse from coughing.

He slid her a sideways glance. "I escorted ye out of a burning buildin' and that's the best ye can come up with." He looked down at the small oval-shaped frame she held tightly in her hands. "Isn't yer bedroom up those stairs also?" he remarked.

She followed his eyes with a surprised look at the frame in her hands. "A picture of my dear mother, I couldn't leave it behind."

The dark of night kept her face in shadow, but he imagined the regal woman's face to be flush with embarrassment. His writer's instincts told him there was more to this story than what the Superior revealed to him.

"After ye, Reverend Mother. I wouldn't want ye to get lost again," Shawn stated, his arm sweeping in a wide gesture in front of him.

Snead stepped in front of him just as he was about to leave the convent grounds. "Why am I not surprised to see ye here?" Shawn stated.

"Thought you might like a souvenir of the convent." Snead's gloved hands tossed a silver tumbler toward him.

Shawn caught the elaborate cup in his hands, the heat of which scorched his skin, causing him to drop it immediately.

When he snapped his head up, ready to do bodily damage to the man he once called boss, Snead was gone.

"A friend of yours, Mr. Fraser?" the Reverend Mother asked.

"Not anymore," Shawn stated, clenching his teeth against the blistering pain.

CHAPTER ELEVEN

In the sultry morning air, Brianna walked along the smoldering remains of the convent. She stared at the heap of ashes where the monastery once stood proudly on top of Mount Benedict. A wall of brick stood alone among the ruins, the only remnant of the building she called home.

"Bri, are ye all right, lass? I knew I shouldn't have allowed ye to come with me. 'Tis too dreadful to see what hatred can do."

"I'm fine, just a little shaken. I needed to come with you to prove to myself that last night really happened. It's still hard to believe the convent's gone even while I stand here looking at it. I've no home to come back to."

"Bri, let me take ye back to the boarding house," Shawn began, his arm ushering her gently to the carriage nearby. He still felt her life was in danger anywhere in this town, especially at the sight of such violence.

He swallowed back the guilt he felt at his involvement with Snead – one of the catalysts of the riot. A year ago, he would have cheered at the burning of a convent and stood front row to watch the flames consume the building, like the people of this town. Now, he saw how hate destroyed. Something had changed for him last night in that fire. Instead of rejoicing, anger simmered deep inside him. Brianna, the children, and the other nuns came close to being harmed. They weren't faceless Catholics anymore.

Shawn turned around at the sound of horses galloping toward them. He drew his gun out of his holster and pushed Brianna behind him.

The men came to a stop in front of them. One man leaned his body forward, his hands resting comfortably on the saddle horn, unperturbed by the gun he held aimed at his head.

"I was told that I could find a Mr. Shawn Fraser here," the man with the badge on his shirt drawled.

"I'm Shawn Fraser. What might ye want with me, sheriff?"

"I've come to escort you into town for questioning before the committee about the riot that took place here last night," the sheriff stated.

"And if I refuse to come?"

"My deputies would need to detain you, any way they saw fit," the man warned, intentionally shifting his hand to the holster of his gun.

Brianna could no longer remain silent. She stepped out from behind Shawn, hands on hips. "My husband helped us all out of the convent last night, nuns, children, and even the Reverend Mother," she stated with a nod.

"Mrs. Fraser, we have reason to believe that your husband did much more than help last night. Talk is he threw the first torch that began the fire," the sheriff stated.

Her hand came up to cover her mouth. Her eyes glanced up at her husband's rigid face, memory of the story he wrote still fresh in her mind.

"Bri, 'tis not like the man says. I came to find ye, remember? Ye were upset over reading the article," Shawn reminded.

She shook her head. "How could you write all that I told you in private?"

"I was never goin' to use it. Ye have to believe me."

The sheriff pulled the gun from Shawn's hand. "Newlyweds, are you?" the sheriff remarked with an easy smile.

"Go back to the boarding house and wait for me there, Bri. Promise me you'll go straight there."

When she didn't answer, he turned and went with the men without a struggle. She held her head high, her face blank of emotion as her husband rode off, but as soon as the group was out of sight, she wrapped her arms around her body and gave in to the anguish that felt like a knife twisted deep into her heart. Her body slid to the ground, her knees collapsing under the weight of her sorrow.

It all made sense now – Shawn's hate for Catholics, the story he wrote, why he lied to her. How could her husband be so cruel as to put all the people that she loved in danger? *What sort of monster was she married to?*

On shaky legs and with strength she didn't know she possessed, she climbed up into the carriage and lightly slapped the leather strap onto the horses' backs. They trotted down the road toward town.

She lifted her chin high. First, she'd seek out Father McBrien and quickly end her farce of a marriage. Then, she'd move into the Sisters of Charity Convent with Mother, Sister Mary Clarence, and Sister Mary Louise and wipe out all memory of Mr. Shawn Fraser.

On the outskirts of town, she pulled back on the reins of the horses, stunned at the sight on the side of the road. Three bodies hung by their necks, swaying gently beneath the branch of a large oak tree. Shawn had told her that several pirates were caught last week and brought to trial, but he had neglected to tell her about the hanging.

Her body shuddered as she traveled past the tree. She said a quick prayer for the souls of the dead men and wondered if her husband would be the next to swing from that tree.

Before the horses crossed the Charlestown bridge, a crudely written sign posted at the entrance drew her attention. It warned against giving information about the burning of the convent or testifying against anyone involved in the affair. *How deeply was her husband embroiled in this hate?*

She pushed away any thoughts of Shawn's welfare to the back of her mind and refused to waste another minute on him. As soon as she found Father McBrien, her marriage would be over, and the life she was meant to lead would begin.

Her breath caught in her throat when a band of men rode toward her, the speed of their horses kicking up clouds of dirt into the air. As they neared, her hands gripped the reins of the horses, ready to race away in the opposite direction. Then she relaxed and waved her hands against the dust kicked up in front of her as they rode swiftly past. She swiveled in her seat and watched the men make their way up the road toward the convent.

She bit down on her lip to stifle her outcry at the cruel act she was witnessing. The men tore apart what was left of the gardens and anything else that was in sight. Savagely, they stamped through the flowers and vineyard, pulling up plants and throwing them into the air. The vines so lovingly caressed to produce such tasty grapes destroyed in a few short minutes. The abundant flowers in multitude of colors crushed to the ground without a second thought. Was it not enough that they destroyed the convent and now they came back to dance on its grave? What sort of cruel beings would do that?

Her face heated up with frustration when she heard the rude comments shouted into the air with glee. Never in her life did she feel such anger toward any man. She gulped back a sob when she realized her husband could have been one of them.

Shawn sat before a panel of thirty-eight men chosen to be on a committee set up to investigate the burning of the convent. He recognized most of them to be prominent businessmen in town. Not one of the men that sat before him was Catholic. That should've made him feel good about the situation but instead left a sour taste in his mouth.

One man stood and stepped toward him. "Your name?"

"Shawn Fraser."

"Are you a Catholic, Mr. Fraser?" the man continued.

"If you knew me, sir, you would know how ridiculous a question that is to ask me. No, I am not," Shawn answered, shaking his head.

The man shuffled papers before him. "But you are married to one of the women from the convent?"

Shawn moved uncomfortably in his seat. It seemed that the committee did their homework. "Yes, I am, Miss Brianna Lawrence."

"Did you marry her to help her escape the convent, sir?" the man asked, clearly confused.

Shawn stared directly at the man until he looked away. "How does my private life have anything to do with the fire?"

"It concerns us if there is ample motive that supports the evidence we have found on you."

"Which is?" Shawn asked, arms crossed firmly in front of him.

"Several men saw you go into the building on the night of the fire. It was only a matter of time before the first floor began to burn. Doc Carlson told us he treated your hand for a burn on the night of the fire."

"I've not to dispute being at the fire that night. I needed to find my wife, she was upset, and I knew she would go back to the convent since it was her home for many years," Shawn stated.

"Mrs. Benson also told us you arrived back early from your holiday with your new wife. Was there a reason why you arrived back to Charlestown on the day before the riots occurred?"

"Business drew me back to town," Shawn replied.

"Business at the newspaper that you worked?"

"Aye," Shawn replied.

The chairman stood up and walked over to him. "Mr. Fraser, I need to be honest with you here. So far, your answers have lacked the truth in accordance with other eyewitness accounts. Your boss, Mr. Henry Snead, painted us a much different picture of your situation. He told us of your hatred for all Catholics and your need to destroy them.

"It wasn't until you came into town that the good folks here grew suspicious about the goings on in the convent. Mr. Snead even told us the fact that you got yourself hired to do work around the convent, inside and out, to get a better look inside the place.

"I'm thinking you couldn't help but take a shining to one of those lonely women up there on the hill. And your conscience wouldn't let her stay in the very building you planned to torch, so you married her and took her as far away from town as possible, then turned around and rushed back into town to do the dirty deed."

"*Mr.* Snead is a liar," Shawn said, his eyes narrowing on his former boss, sitting among the investigative committee.

"Are you calling one of our finest businessmen in town a liar, Mr. Fraser?" the man asked flabbergasted.

Shawn looked directly at Snead. "Aye, I am."

"Are you asking us to believe you, a total stranger to our little town, over someone that has had a long standing of respect from this community?"

"Aye, I am," Shawn repeated.

"Then I suggest you make yourself comfortable during these proceedings in the accommodations the sheriff has set up for you. Until you are forthright with us about your involvement in this mishap, your love for violence will keep you locked up until your trial begins. And I do need to remind you that this crime is a capital offense, punishable by death."

Shawn shot up from his seat. "You have no solid evidence against me!" he stated irritated, knowing his fate was already sealed.

Angry men stood in front of the cathedral beside the Sisters of Charity convent. Brianna took two steps back and away from the mob, afraid to be seen or recognized as part of the Ursuline convent. Just when she thought a brick would be thrown through the long arched window of the church, a small militia of men appeared from around the corner of the building.

"All of you go back to your homes!" the man in the front of the militia demanded.

"Who the hell are you to tell us this?" one of the men in the mob shouted back.

"Independent Light Infantry Company, formed by the committee investigating the burning of the convent last night. We'll lock up the whole lot of you if you don't disperse quickly enough," the man in charge warned.

Brianna heard the men grumbling under their breaths. Eventually, they did walk away, but she feared this was not the end of their anger toward the church.

She found Father McBrien at the altar of the church, deep in prayer. He turned toward her with a wide smile.

"I'm sorry to disturb you, Father McBrien. I know this isn't a good time," Brianna began.

"What is it, child?"

"I've recently found out that my husband was at the center of the riots that destroyed the Ursuline convent. His deep hatred for Catholics made him...." She stopped speaking, her throat too choked with tears.

The elderly priest ushered her to a pew and sat beside her. "Are you sure he was involved? Sometimes when we're upset, our minds don't think as clearly as we'd like them."

"The sheriff took him away this morning and told me himself that he had reason to believe that Shawn threw the first torch to start the fire last night. I can't stay married to someone like that."

When she looked up, all color drained from his face.

"Father McBrien, I know how trying this time is for you with everything that has happened and those men trying to get in to destroy *this* church too. I shouldn't have come here with my problems."

He rubbed his hand down his face and sat back on the pew. "Nonsense, child. Just give me a minute to think." He closed his eyes. "In order to get an annulment to your marriage, I must ask you a delicate question. Did you have marital relations with your husband?" the elderly priest asked discreetly.

"If you're asking if we slept together, the answer is no," Brianna answered, the heat of her embarrassment brightening her cheeks.

"Good, then I will draft the papers needed and bring them to the jail for your husband to sign. As soon as that is done, I'll file the papers with the church authorities, and your marriage will be dissolved." He took both of her hands into his and looked deep into her eyes. "You're doing the right thing."

"Of course, I could never stay married to a man so horrible," she replied.

"Even if you could turn him toward Catholicism," he stated.

"I don't know why he married me in the first place or why Mother Superior allowed it," Brianna stated, confused, her emotions tangled into tight hard knots.

"Maybe his heart and mind think differently," the priest added.

"Even if that was true, he still intended to harm everyone at the convent. I'll be glad when the papers are filed and I can go on to become the nun I always dreamt I'd be." She blinked away tears, refusing to shed one more drop for a man that meant nothing to her.

Father McBrien's sharp eyes glanced over at her. "I can see by your words that your heart and mind are thinking differently also." He patted her knee. "We were both fooled by Mr. Shawn Fraser."

Shawn watched Snead's cocky form stroll into the sheriff's office.

"Came to see me hang by your words, Snead?" Shawn stated, his fists tightening around the bars of his cell, the sting of the wounds on his hands a forever reminder of the calculating mind of the man in front of him.

His boss pulled the cigar from his mouth. "I warned you that I don't take kindly to threats made by one of my own reporters."

"As soon as I get out of here, I'm going to hunt ye down," Shawn promised.

"Don't think that's going to be anytime soon. I have several friends in town that don't take kindly to a Catholic sympathizer. No, not at all," he said, shaking his head. "Heard they also told that special committee that you arranged and organized the entire event. No, you won't be coming out any time soon."

"I'll come back for you, even if it's from my grave," Shawn threatened.

"I'm afraid you might have to since word around town is that your case is never going to get to court. There's a bunch of Irishmen threatening to come over from Boston to take the law into their own hands. They want to make sure that the culprit that is responsible for the burning of their beloved convent pays for his crime."

"Another headline for your paper?" Shawn asked.

Snead shrugged his shoulders and stuck the cigar back in his mouth. "My men told me they saw your wife riding out of town," Snead announced. Shawn's head snapped up at his words.

Shawn gripped the bars of his cell. "What have ye done with her, Snead!"

Snead leaned in real close to Shawn's face. "I'm willing to do whatever it takes to stop the poison of Catholicism from spreading into Charlestown," Snead announced. "I wouldn't go worrying about that pretty little wife of yours. The boys will be taking real good care of her."

Shawn shoved his hands through the opening of the bars of his cell and groped for Snead's neck, his need to kill the man pulsed through his veins. Snead jumped back out of his reach, threw back his head, and laughed. He laughed so hard that his cigar fell out of his crooked mouth onto the floor.

"Snead, time's up. Get out of here," the sheriff stated, walking into the room.

Shawn paced his cell like a crazed animal in a trap. "I've got to get out of here, sheriff! He's kidnapped my wife!"

"The way I heard it told, she decided to leave town on her own to get away from you, so don't go throwing accusations out too easily,

Fraser, or I won't allow you another visitor," the sheriff stated.

To Shawn's utter surprise, his father, dressed in his black suit and white collar, stepped out from behind the sheriff. Father McBrien didn't say a word until the sheriff left them alone.

His father's eyes narrowed with contempt when he looked down his nose at him through the bars of his cell, which only provoked his ire.

Shawn strode across the room frustrated. "Don't give me that holier-than-thou look!" he remarked before his father had the chance to speak.

"You'll do Brianna a favor by signing these papers," his father stated.

Shawn grabbed the papers his father stuck through the opening in the bars. "She's annulling the marriage without giving me the chance to explain?" *Dammit, he needed more than ever to get out of here!*

He crumpled the parchment in his hands. "Couldn't wait to get rid of me, could you?"

His father shook his head. "You've brought this on yourself. She deserves better than you."

Shawn tucked away his quick retort and gripped the bars in front of him in frustration. "Snead and his culprits have her."

"Snead – meaning your employer? I knew if she was mixed up with you, something like this would happen. How could you?" his father shouted.

"Look, I don't care what ye think I did or didn't do, I need to get out of here!" Shawn explained, irritation lining every word he spoke.

His father looked over at him sadly, ignoring Shawn's tone of voice. "You did all this to get back at me, didn't you? Your cruel revenge not only hurt your wife, the sisters at the convent, but also frightened innocent children. Their fear of that night will stay in their memories forever. Forever!"

Shawn combed his hands through his hair. "I don't care if you believe me or not, but I didn't do this. I'd never do anything to jeopardize Brianna or any of those people. I had a story to tell that would have shut down the convent without a fire or riot to destroy it."

"Now, what nonsense are you talking about?" his father asked.

Shawn hesitated before he spoke, his voice cold and hard. "Brianna told me of the Reverend Mother's drinking after Sister Mary Margaret died. If I wanted to destroy the convent, I'd have given Snead that story, and the doors to that school would have been closed forever. You and I both know that."

His father mulled over the significance of his words while he paced the outside of his cell. He lifted his bushy brows with a shake to his head. "I never knew for sure. I always suspected something was amiss with the Reverend Mother."

"So ye can see that I could have used the information if I chose to, but I did not. I need to get out of here and find my wife, *your* daughter-in-law. You've got to help me," Shawn urged.

Their eyes connected – man to man rather than Catholic to Protestant. For a second, the hard line drawn in the dirt suddenly blurred.

"I'll see what I can do," his father said.

His thoughts were interrupted when the sheriff's door opened once again, and to his utter amazement, his two aunts marched into the building, their arms loaded with items.

"Ladies, what are ye doin' here?" Shawn asked, incredulous.

"Now, that's a ridiculous statement, isn't, sister? We came to visit ye," Aunt Bea stated as if he had lost his mind.

Aunt Liddea just stood in front of the cell and shook her head. "Oh, my," she said, her hands full of clothes. "He looks so thin, sister," she remarked, her eyes taking in the length of him.

"Are they feeding ye, Shawn? I brought your favorite – potato casserole. Even put in some of those green apples you like chopped up real small. You always did have a sweet tooth," Aunt Bea remarked.

"Ladies, why are you here? I left you in Halifax more than a week ago," Shawn stated.

Aunt Liddea cleared her throat and tilted her head toward his father, who was openly staring at his aunts. "This is my Aunt Bea and Aunt Liddea. They were jus about to answer how they came to be in Charlestown so quickly after I left them."

Aunt Bea placed the casserole dish on the sheriff's desk and turned back toward Shawn with her hands set squarely on her hips. "No need to take that tone of voice with us, Shawn. It's your own fault you're in this jail cell. Starting a fire is a serious sin. Sister and I knew you were aiming for trouble every time you put down those Catholics. We tried to explain that father of yours was one bad apple in the bunch and it didn't mean they were all bad," Aunt Bea stated, glancing over at McBrien with an apologetic smile, "but you wouldn't listen. Instead, you took the law into your own hands, and look at what it got you?" Aunt Bea scolded.

"This is Father McBrien, the *bad* apple," Shawn repeated.

Aunt Bea's hand flew to her mouth. "He's your f-a-t-h-e-r?" she whispered, spelling out the word.

"He knows how to spell, Aunt Bea," Shawn stated.

"He doesn't look like the monster I always imagined him to be," Aunt Liddea remarked, her eyes studying McBrien.

Shawn cleared his throat and turned his attention to his father. "He and I have come to an understanding, haven't we?"

"Yes, we have, and I'm afraid I must be on my way," his father stated, backing out of the room.

Aunt Liddea stepped forward, drawing herself up in front of Shawn and stated, "Sister and I both decided that you're too young to die and the two of us have had a long enjoyable life. We're going to take the blame for your horrendous actions."

Shawn stood with his mouth open, feeling five years old again and having his aunts explain to his grade school teacher why he was really a good boy and didn't mean to stick Susy's braid in the inkwell.

With an easy smile, his father stated, "He's not convicted yet, ladies. But we do need to get him out of here so he can search for his wife."

Aunt Liddea placed her hands on her hips and turned to Shawn. "You lost your wife? How could you, we sent her on Captain McAndry's ship. We watched her board," Aunt Liddea exclaimed, then covered her mouth when she realized that she said too much.

"I knew you two were behind her following me. How many times have I told you not to interfere in my life?" Shawn asked.

"We're all concerned about Brianna, but there's no need to use harsh words on these two lovely women, who obviously care a great deal about you," his father gently reprimanded, smiling warmly at his aunts before he stepped out of the room.

Shawn rolled his eyes and exhaled a long unsteady breath. "Aunt Bea and Aunt Liddea, I apologize. I'm jus so frustrated sitting in this cell when Brianna needs me!"

Aunt Bea moved close to the bars of the cell and whispered, "Did you realize that man, your *father*, is Catholic?"

"Of course, he's a priest," Shawn replied, just as quietly.

"Are you feeling ill?" Aunt Bea asked concerned.

Aunt Liddea poked her head into the conversation. "What's wrong with the boy?" Her hand automatically reached through the opening between the bars to rest on his forehead.

"He's taken to Catholics," Aunt Bea remarked in disbelief.

Chapter Twelve

Shawn looked up confused when the sheriff swung the door of his cell wide open.

"Seems you made some friends at that Ursuline Convent. Heard the Superior herself came down and spoke to the committee on your behalf. As much as I don't agree with their decision, I have to obey it," the sheriff informed him.

"I'm free to go?" Shawn asked in disbelief.

"You're free, but I'll be watching every move you make, Fraser. Just because a couple of nuns were pressured into telling the committee a bunch of lies, doesn't mean I necessarily believe them."

Shawn started to walk out the front door and hesitated. "That group of Irishmen making their way into town still?"

The sheriff nodded, a slow grin forming on his face. "They'll be sniffing your trail soon enough."

Shawn quietly slipped out the back door of the jail into the darkness of the night. He was shocked to see his father and the Reverend Mother standing in front of him. Confused, Shawn asked, "Why are ye helpin' me?"

The Reverend Mother stepped forward. "We're helping you, Mr. Fraser, because it is the right thing to do. I told the committee that I would sign an affidavit stating the facts as I recalled them. We're all grateful for your help that fateful night," Mother Superior stated with a nod.

Shawn grabbed hold of the Reverend Mother's shoulders and to her utter surprise, he kissed her soundly on both cheeks. "Thank ye. I shall never forget the favor ye did by comin' forward and clearin' my name," Shawn vowed.

His father pulled the reins of the horse close. "We're all praying that you'll find Brianna," he stated quietly.

Shawn grabbed hold of the reins. "I'll find her."

Darkness fell like a blanket onto the streets of Charlestown.

Shawn heard the rambunctious Irish crowd gathered at the edge of town and suspected that they were equipped with rope tied into a custom-fit loop for his neck. He turned the horse into the opposite direction and made his way out of town.

Brianna's eyes glanced around the old abandoned cabin, careful to lean away from the cobwebs that hung from the walls and ceiling. Leaves scattered across the dirt floor. The film of dirt caked onto the small window by the door was so thick and yellow that it was impossible to see through the glass, except for a small cracked opening on the bottom right corner.

Quietly, she peeked through the crack in the window when the sound of voices drifted into the cabin. Four men originally brought her to the cabin, staying through the night. Two of the men left early the next morning.

"How long is he going to keep me out here?" Brianna recognized the voice of the man that stayed at the cabin with her during the day. His voice sounded impatient, and she assumed he didn't like to be cooped up in the woods any more than she did.

"Snead says he's waiting for Fraser to hang for the murder of his wife," another replied.

Brianna clenched the front of her dress, twisting it within her hands while her mind pondered the man's unbelievable words. *Shawn was going to hang for her murder?*

The first voice startled her thoughts. "Who's going to kill the nun?"

"She's not a nun, stupid. She's his wife," the first voice replied.

"Nun or not, I've never killed no woman before. I admit it felt good to be paid to use my fists on Fraser, but a woman is another story."

"You get a taste for it after a while," another said before she heard him spit on the ground. She shivered at the tone of his voice.

"Who'll listen to her once Fraser is dead? Why not just leave her up here, locked up in this cabin?" the first voice whined.

Brianna's thoughts raced to Shawn and the terrible predicament he was put in because of her. Until now, she thought only her life was in danger.

Shawn remembered Snead mentioning the cabin to him, his grandfather's old place. It was deep in the hills, miles from town, and if not for the fact that Snead had given him the exact location of the abandoned cabin, he would never have known how to find it.

Fear drove him to ride hard to find her before it was too late. He should have never allowed her to come back into town with him. His normally rational sensible mind became clouded every time he was around his wife.

The feeling in his gut made him push the horse harder, faster, worried about what he might find at the cabin. He followed the creek out of town for at least two miles, and there he picked up a trail toward the dense hills outside of town.

Anger pulsed through his veins, revenge at the forefront of his mind. Never had he felt such revulsion toward his boss as now. If he touched one precious red hair on Brianna's sweet head, he would tear the man apart, limb by limb.

"Whoa," he whispered to the horse, pulling back on the reins when the abandoned cabin came into sight.

He wasn't surprised when he saw the smoke drift up from the chimney. Following his gut was something he came to rely on over the years when investigating a story.

He approached the cabin from the south, leaving his horse in a grove farther up the trail and then backtracking on foot to the cabin. His hand hovered over his gun, ready to take out any man near his wife.

Slowly, with his back against the wall, he rounded the building, sliding over to a small window at the back of the cabin. He peered inside, his eyes locking on the scene before him. A minute later, he pulled away from the window, shaking his head.

Brianna sat at a table in the center of the small room with one man sitting on either side of her. The men looked familiar, stone faces with long, dirt-encrusted hair.

He'd wager the one on the right of Brianna to be the same man that slit his arm a few weeks back. His hand rubbed his jaw, remembering the other lucky punch of the second man in the room. It looked like he'd get a second chance at teaching them a lesson.

That wasn't what made him shake his head though. It was what they were doing that made him smile. These hardened men, who could have had the word *mean* written across their forehead, had their heads bowed low in prayer while his petite wife prayed over the measly amount of food that sat untouched on the table before them. Brianna never ceased to amaze him.

With the butt of his gun, Shawn tapped on the pane of the window and waited for the back door to open. When it did, he yanked the man out, slammed the handle of his gun against the back of his head, and waited for the second man to investigate the matter.

Slowly, the door of the cabin opened a second time, the barrel of a gun extended first. He was just about to grab the gun when it went off unexpectedly, and the man fell to the floor with the door swinging wide open behind him.

His wife stood over him, her hands gripping the handle of an iron kettle, her green eyes full of remorse, looking down at the man.

Her hand automatically came up to form the sign of the cross before her eyes rose from the body up to him.

"Did I kill him?" she asked softly, her knees dropping to the man's side. "I only meant to stop him."

Shawn slowly shook his head and took a step toward her.

She jumped up and took two steps back, lifting the heavy kettle she held in her hands. "Stay away from me."

"Bri, I've come to get ye. Put the kettle down," he stated in a calm reasonable voice. "'Tis all over. Ye've done a fine job of it," he assured her, taking another step toward her.

"Don't step any closer, Shawn, or I'll have to hurt you too," she warned, her hands wavering under the weight of the kettle.

"I'm here to rescue ye, lass, not hurt ye."

"I'm not married to you anymore, so I don't need to listen to you."

He winced a bit in anticipation of her reply, absently rubbing the back of his neck. "Now that's something ye and I need to discuss. I never did get to signin' those papers ye sent to me while I was in jail."

"You destroyed my home and the home of all my sister nuns and frightened those poor children to death and still expect me to stay married to you?" she screamed at a fevered pitch. Her hand slapped over her mouth, ashamed at her own lack of control. She breathed in deeply and in a much calmer voice whispered, "I could never stay married to a monster like you."

"I've much explainin' to do, I know that, lass, but not here. Let me take ye home, where we can talk about all that happened and my role in it. Though I swear to ye right now on me own mother's grave that it wasn't me that lit the first match to set the fire."

At the click of a cocked gun, Shawn's eyes glanced to the side, only to feel the pressure of a barrel pressed against the middle of his back.

"He's right on that point, Mrs. Fraser. I'll take credit for that fact. I threw the first torch and many more after that and took full enjoyment watching the flames grow," Snead announced with a sneer. "Always knew this old cabin would come in handy someday."

"Let my wife go, she has no part in this. Yer gripe is with me, not her."

"Your affection for your *Catholic* wife is so touching, but I'm afraid things have gone much too far along for me to allow her to live. My headlines are already set and ready to print. *Reporter destroys convent, then hunts down and kills wife-nun.* So you see, it would be much too much work to change the outcome of the story now," Snead said, shaking his head, making a tsk-ing sound.

"She's an innocent in all this, surely even ye can see that!" Shawn insisted.

"No Catholic is innocent. This world will be a better place when every single one of them is dead. Not that I didn't enjoy the spin you put on this story, Fraser. I needed a fool to take the blame for the fire, and in you walked. Anyone that walks into my newspaper looking for a job has some sort of hatred towards Catholics, some sort of wrong to right against them. You were so blinded by your hatred that you stepped right into the role I needed you to play. It just didn't seem neighborly of me to have one of our own townspeople hung for such a mishap."

"Ye set me up from the start, ye lousy bastard!" Shawn burst out before he lunged at Snead.

A bullet whistled past Shawn's right ear and hit Snead in the middle of his forehead. Shock crossed Snead's face before he fell forward onto the ground.

The sheriff stepped out from behind the cabin, placing his gun back in his holster. He knelt beside Snead's body. "He's dead."

Brianna bent down beside the body next to Snead, her face pale. "Are you sure he's not dead? I shouldn't have hit him so hard with the kettle, but I acted without thinking because I was afraid he was about to shoot you with his gun. I've never harmed another living soul," she babbled.

Shawn's arm came around her. "Jus unconscious, not dead. And Snead is scum that needed to be taken care of before he did more harm."

She hugged her trembling arms against her body. "They were misdirected men, following the wrong path in life. I talked with them. They have families. What did you do with Tom?"

"Tom?" Shawn asked.

"The first man that came out of the cabin?"

He hesitated, not wanting to tell his innocent wife that the man she affectionately called Tom was lying unconscious on the other side of the building.

The sheriff stepped forward before he had the chance to answer. "Heard the whole thing, Fraser. Seems I did have the story wrong. I'll explain to the committee what happened here today."

"I'd be obliged, Sheriff," Shawn replied.

She walked with Shawn down the road a bit to where he left his horse tied to a tree. "I owe you an apology."

He glanced at her out of the corner of his eye. "Aye, ye do."

"I'm sorry for not trusting your word. You once told me you were an honest man. I should have believed you."

"Bri, I *was* tempted to use the story I wrote."

She shook her head. "Tempted, but you would never have printed it."

"How do you know that?" he asked, faintly amused.

"You're not like Snead or any of the other men that ransacked the convent. You never could be." Her deep green eyes grew serious. "It all makes sense to me now. You knew there was going to be trouble at the convent, didn't you? You married me to get me out of the convent and away from harm. Only a good man would do something so selfless. I owe you my life."

Shawn cleared his throat and lifted her body onto the horse. His eyes held hers when he stated, "Likewise, lass. If ye didn't bandage me up that dark night, I wouldn't be here today."

"So we're even then."

"Aye," he replied, straddling the horse behind her.

CHAPTER THIRTEEN

Brianna tried not to think about the date. She used all her energy today to concentrate on forgetting all about what tomorrow would mean to her and her marriage. The more she sought to forget it, the more it stuck in her mind like the uncomfortable feel of a pebble slipped into the soles of her shoes.

As much as she might want to forget it, she couldn't avoid the fact that today was the last day of the month, and there was nothing she could do to change it.

She finally gave up and closed the Bible Shawn had so generously given to her. The precious holy book, covered in leather, she would treasure always. The old stories warmed her heart, but today her mind wouldn't stay focused on the words.

She appreciated the loving way the aunts fussed over her as soon as she arrived back in Halifax. With each day that passed, she became more and more depressed at the thought of leaving them. Even more troubling was the fact that Shawn hardly ever left her side, which only made her love him more.

"Are ye sorry we traveled back up north?" Shawn asked. "I can see the wheels turning in yer head. Do ye wish to talk about what's botherin' ye?"

She opened her mouth to reply, but every time she began, the words stuck in her throat. She realized that if she voiced her feelings aloud, it would only make him feel uncomfortable that he couldn't return them.

"Tell me, Bri," he urged, frustration beginning to edge its way into his voice.

She wouldn't have detected that smidgen of frustration a month ago, she thought, which only confirmed how much she had learned about him in the past couple of weeks. Like the way he rolled his eyes every time one of his aunts threatened to trim the length of his russet-colored hair. How he never buttoned the top two buttons of his shirt because it made him feel uncomfortable. Or the fact that he'd pull out pen and paper at the oddest times to scribble together a string of words to expertly express a thought or event.

When the wind slammed the shutters of the house against its frame, she jumped back, startled but relieved for the distraction. Thunder rumbled above their heads, right before the wind swept torrents of rain slashing against the house.

Brianna stood with fingers pressed against the windowpane, her eyes watching drops of water bounce off the glass. The soothing rhythm comforting her troubled mind.

"Are ye worried about singing in church tomorrow? Yer voice is a blessing from God. 'Tis a shame not to share it with everyone," he said.

"No, I'm a little nervous about tomorrow, but not worried. Those people feel like family to me now. I love them all." She burst into tears and ran upstairs to their bedroom, shutting the door firmly behind her.

"Bri!" Shawn shouted, following her up the stairs.

She quickly closed the door behind her, slid her body to the floor, and wept. How could she be in such a predicament, she sobbed. How could she have fallen in love with a man that didn't want or need a real wife? Hadn't he been brutally honest from the beginning when he stressed repeatedly to her that all he wanted was a *wife in name only*?

"Bri, let me in," Shawn urged from the other side of the door.

"I'm suddenly tired. Let me rest a while, please," she choked out, struggling to speak through her anguish.

Could she not do anything right? Was this the way she was to repay his kindness, by complicating his life with a wife that was in love with him? She knew it wasn't right to infringe on his generosity any longer. It was time for her to free him so he could find a wife he truly loved, not one he married to repay a debt.

After experiencing life outside of the convent, she came to the sad conclusion that she didn't have the true calling to be a nun. Rather her fear of leaving the confines of the convent clouded her judgement, making it seem like the life of a nun was right for her. In Nova Scotia, she felt like she could spread her wings for the first time in her life and become the person she was meant to be, the person God intended her to be. Singing was a start for her, maybe even a way to earn a living.

She knew that Shawn was too good of a man to kick her out of his aunts' house, so it was up to her to do it for him. She sensed his need to move on with his life, his talent with words too exceptional to lie in waste. If only her feelings for him had not deepened, then it wouldn't be so difficult to walk away.

Slowly, she stood up, pulled her small suitcase from under the bed, and began packing her dresses. She remembered the morning Shawn had walked into the kitchen of his aunts' cottage, arms filled with an array of dresses, which he admitted to have ordered especially for her. She thought about how it must have looked, a big man like Shawn, walking into the dress shop in town, browsing through the different textured material, picking out this and that color to please her.

When she finished packing, she took a shaky breath, wiped her eyes with the back of her hand, and tried to calm herself before she ventured back downstairs and faced Shawn.

Slowly, she descended the stairs, hoping that her broken heart wouldn't be detected by anyone. It would only cause them pain to know how hard it was for her to leave them all.

"Did you have a nice nap, dear?" Aunt Liddea asked, looking up from the knitting on her lap.

"Nap?" Brianna asked confused.

"Yes, right before Shawn left, he told me you were a bit tired and were taking a little rest upstairs," Aunt Liddea stated, her fingers busy with yarn and needles.

"Where did Shawn go?" Brianna asked, her red eyes carefully averted.

"Joe Stevens asked if he could help him get out a cow stuck in a trench by his farm. He's afraid the animal will die if the storm hits hard and it ends up being washed away by the creek overflowing."

Brianna walked back to the stairs, her heart fluttering an erratic beat. She knew what she needed to do in the next hour and hoped she had the courage to do so.

"Are you feeling all right, dear? You look a little pale." Aunt

Liddea set down her knitting needles to study her.

Brianna forced herself to relax and even managed a faint smile. "Yes, I think I'm still a little tired. Maybe I'll lie down a while longer," Brianna added with a forced yawn. It was only a little white lie, she told herself. Better that than take advantage of these good people's generosity any longer.

She moved quietly down the back staircase and out the door, her suitcase firmly in hand. With a last tearful glance at the house and her life there, she entered the barn, hitched up the horses to the carriage, and left.

She told herself that she was never really a true wife to Shawn. There were times, she admitted, when she thought he was growing to love her, but now she knew that she was confusing kindness with love. The kisses they shared, all signs of affection, not love.

She tossed back the wet strands of hair and strained to see the road in front of her through the thick rain. Maybe she should have waited for the storm to subside a bit before venturing out, but by then Shawn might have returned, and that would ruin all of her plans. No, she would rather brave the rains, mud, and winds than put her husband in an uncomfortable position.

Shawn was still young and *deserved* to marry a woman he loved, a woman of his choosing, not one to which he felt beholden. Someone he could give his whole heart to, raise a family together, grow old together, she thought with a tearful sigh. His debt to her was more than paid for by all the kindness he had showered on her over the past month. Now, she would return the favor and walk out of his life forever.

Joe Stevens dug a trench around the animal, hoping to free him. Shawn continued to pull on the animal, though his mind was on another entirely different matter.

The promise he made to his wife on the day they married was in the forefront of his mind. Today was the last day of the month, tomorrow he would escort her back to Charlestown. If anything, he was a man of his word.

He knew she wanted that black veil, knew it from the first time they met, even held her when she cried over the lack of it. So he was determined not to let any foolish notions enter his head today about her changing her mind over such an important decision. For whatever reason, their lives had been thrown together for the month of August, and now he needed to return her to the church.

When Shawn insisted that she accompany him back to Halifax until the end of the month, it wasn't because he expected any more harm to come to her. No, quite the opposite was true. He admitted to himself that after all they had been through, he wasn't ready to give her up. He wanted to spend time with her, even if it was only a few short weeks before returning her to the convent and signing those annulment papers he had stashed away in his satchel. It was selfish of him, he knew, but after the fire and kidnapping and all the worry that she caused him, he felt he deserved this time alone with her.

After one last strong tug, the cow pulled free, and he hurried off toward home and Brianna. He reminded himself that he would not pressure her in any way. Some things were better left unsaid.

Brianna clutched the straps of the horses, steering the carriage as best she could in the middle of the drenching rains. No one had a clue as to where she was and wouldn't until later today. She hoped by that time she would be aboard a ship and halfway down the coast.

It was better this way, without making the aunts or Shawn feel obligated to have her stay there any longer. Time to begin her new life.

With her body hunched over against the icy winds, she fought to keep hold of the reins. The horses slowly trotted through the mud-soaked roads, which were quickly getting worse by the minute. When she was ready to give up all hope of ever reaching town, the buildings on the docks came into sight.

Shielding her body against the driving rains, she jumped down from the rig and hurried into the only building that looked to be open. A sense of relief followed her into the establishment. The room lit by a scattering of candles didn't shed much light on a stormy day like today. Numerous tables cluttered the small space filled with men, all of which stopped and turned toward her when she entered.

"'Ave ye lost yer way, Miss?" the man behind the counter asked.

"No," she answered quietly.

He motioned her over to the counter.

"We don't get many woman like you in here," he informed her.

She felt her face heat up with embarrassment. "What do you mean women like me? I know I'm soaking wet and my hair is a tangled mop on top of my head, but if you direct me to a dressing room, I'll straighten out my appearance."

The man shook his head, looking uncomfortable. "Proper women. We're used to women without morals, if ya get what I mean," he said with eyebrows raised high.

"I'm not sure I've ever met anyone like that—" she began, but she was interrupted by a voice behind her.

"And ye won't anytime soon," the voice assured her.

She swiveled around at the sound of the familiar voice. "Captain McAndry, just the person I was looking for."

"You're not going to keep that pretty filly all to yourself, are ya now, McAndry?" a man sitting at a table beside Brianna remarked.

"Aye, I am." Captain McAndry stated to the room at large. "The lass is the wife of a good friend, so stop your staring as if she's about to pop wings or such." Then Captain McAndry turned back to Brianna and ushered her to a table in the back of the room.

"Where's Shawn?"

"He's helping Joe Stevens pull a cow out of the mud," she answered, lowering her eyes.

He lifted her chin, his stern eyes meeting hers. "I know Shawn would never have ye travel alone in the middle of this storm, so what's going on, lass? Tell me the truth."

"I need to travel down the coast, and I thought you might be able to help me," Brianna began.

Captain McAndry crossed his arms and narrowed his eyes. "What's the boy done?"

"Nothing, I just need to get away," Brianna stated, her face flush with the lie.

"I'm not as stupid as ye might think," the captain stated, his eyes studying her from beneath bushy brows.

"Oh, I'm so sorry. I didn't mean for you to think that at all. You've always been so kind." Tears balanced on the rims of her eyes but she refused to let them fall. "I have to leave before he finds me."

Captain McAndry leaned in close to her. "Tell me why, lass. I hate to see ye this upset."

Brianna exhaled a breath. "I'm leaving Shawn so that he can be free to marry someone that he truly loves. Our marriage was temporary from the start, he told me so himself. He married me out of the kindness of his heart, and I will always love him for that."

"I *know* the boy has feelings for ye," Captain McAndry began.

"He's too kind a man not to feel indebted to me since I bandaged him up and cared for him in the convent. Of course, then I didn't know that he was there to investigate a story," she stated with a nod.

"There's history between him and the church."

"Aunt Liddea and Aunt Bea told me the whole sad story of Shawn's mother and what happened to her. I know now why he was at the convent and don't have any ill feelings toward him for it."

"Then why leave him? He'll give ye his heart soon enough."

"I'm afraid he'll give me his heart for all the wrong reasons – out of guilt or out of wanting to do the right thing. He took me out of the convent, and now I'm thinking he probably feels some sort of responsibility toward me because of that."

Brianna covered her face with her hands, not wanting to upset the captain but not able to hold in her tears any longer. A sailor behind her nudged a handkerchief toward her with a sympathetic smile. The barkeep brought her a warm cup of tea and urged her to drink.

Another brawn sailor turned his chair around from his table to hers and stated, "I'll sail ya anywhere you'd like just to stop your tears, Miss."

Brianna blinked back tears. "You've all been so kind. Thank you." Then she burst into tears over the kindness showered on her by strangers.

Captain McAndry awkwardly patted her on the back, and the men beside her tried to console her with comforting words.

CHAPTER FOURTEEN

The violent storm matched Shawn's dark mood. What would have possessed her to go out in such weather? Branches, leaves, shutters, anything not nailed down found itself swept up by the violent winds. Thunder rumbled overhead, slashes of lightning streaked across the darkened skies, making his horse skittish to plunge its hooves through the deep mud of the road.

The more he thought about her leaving, the angrier he became. How dare she risk her life out in this mess on the last day of the month? Did she have so little trust in him that she feared he wouldn't allow her to leave tomorrow? And he thought, struggling to control his anger and the reins of the nervous horse below him, was she in such a rush to leave that she couldn't give him the courtesy of a proper farewell?

Something inside him snapped. How dare she leave him, when he had done everything in his power over the past month to keep her from harm? Didn't he race through a burning building to search for her? He'd lay down his life for her. Didn't she realize how much he *loved* her?

He was so startled by his words that he nearly fell off his own horse. Did he actually say he loved Brianna? Never in his wildest dreams did he think that what he felt toward her could be love, desire and caring maybe, but love?

He turned his face up to the sky and allowed the rain to drench his misery. The pain that seared through his heart at the thought of never seeing her again felt too intense, too real not to be love.

Brianna stood motionless by the window, watching the seas swell up against the gusts of wind, swirling its white frothy tips. Waves lapped water over the docks. Ships swayed and pulled against the ropes that secured them.

Captain McAndry told her that the earliest they could sail out would be tomorrow morning, which only made her worry more. She needed to leave before Shawn discovered that she was here.

Emotionally drained, she sat back in her chair. Captain McAndry placed a wool blanket over her shoulders while she sipped the warm liquid set in front of her. One sailor after another tried to cheer her up with humorous tales to distract her from the storm and her impatience to leave, but it only made her eyes fill with tears over the compassion shown her.

"Ye've need of a rest. Follow me," Captain McAndry stated.

He ushered her to a room in the back of the pub. An oil-burning lamp set on a small nightstand lit the tiny room. It didn't take much coaxing by the captain to get her to lie down on the narrow bed. As soon as her head hit the pillow, she fell into a deep sleep.

Shawn threw back the door of the pub with vengeance. His eyes wildly scanned the room, looking for any sign of her. He strode in, body drenched, his hair wet and flung back over his head, his stance ready for a fight.

He flipped over tables and chairs, shoving aside men like a crazed lunatic, which was what he felt like ever since he found out that Brianna had left him. When he saw the horses and carriage out front, he knew he'd found her.

"Where the hell is she?" he shouted into the silence of the room.

"You're a madman, no wonder she'll have no part of you!" the barkeep replied.

He struggled to rein in his temper. "Jus tell me where me wife is, or I'll kill every man in here with my own two hands!"

"Aye, like ye could do that in the condition ye're in, lad," a familiar voice stated.

Shawn turned to see McAndry walk into the room from the back hall.

He strode over to him. The old man stood with crossed arms and a stubborn look on his face.

"I want to see her," Shawn stated, his impatience clearly visible.

"Don't think the lass wants to see ye, laddie. Seems she doesn't think her own husband loves her."

"Why would she even care if I did?" Shawn asked. "She came

here to buy passage on a ship, didn't she? To get as far away from me as possible, didn't she?"

McAndry ignored his words. "Told me ye married her out of guilt for what she did for ye. Did ye never think to be honest with the gil, tell her how ye really felt, or don't ye know yerself?"

"'Tis none of yer business, McAndry," Shawn snapped back.

"'Tis now. The lass has had her feelings hurt by ye and is determined to leave ye, for yer own good, she says," McAndry added, with one bushy brow lifted high.

A few men gathered around McAndry when he made to step into the hallway towards the room where Brianna slept.

McAndry shook his head. "The lass only now fell asleep. Give a care and allow her to rest a bit before ye approach her."

Shawn watched the men around him link arms, blocking entry to the hall. He strode to the bar. His innocent, timid wife seemed to have the uncanny knack of drawing the best out of the most cold-hearted bunch of ruffians in town. He could see that she had already won the heart of every man inside this dismal place.

The same men ushered him to a table, pulled up chairs, and sat beside him. For the next hour he was berated about his attitude toward his wife and his lack of sensitivity by these burly men who seemed to have all gone soft at the mention of Brianna's name. It was beginning to irritate him. McAndry stepped in when his patience thinned and he was about to punch out the next man that spoke.

"She won't be easily swayed, lad, I can guarantee that," McAndry stated.

Shawn grunted in reply.

McAndry lifted one eyebrow high, his eyes narrowing on Shawn. "So if you're thinking of pushing your way in and stating the fact that you love her – she won't believe you."

"Why would she care if I love her? The woman was leavin' me, wasn't she?"

Captain McAndry knocked him on the side of his head with the back of his hand. "Think, lad, would the woman make such a fuss if she didn't care for you in return? How can you spend a month together and never talk?"

Shawn rubbed his hand down his weary face. "Brianna has

always wanted to be a nun. She doesn't want me, she only wants the black veil."

"So ye skirted the issue of love all these days, did ye? Certain she'd choose the church over ye?" McAndry asked.

"She ran away, didn't she? Doesn't that prove my point?"

The men sitting around the table shook their heads sympathetically.

"What?" Shawn exclaimed irritated.

A sailor across from Shawn shushed him quiet with a tilt of his head toward Brianna's room.

"If not for the land anchor, I'd gladly be swabbing the deck of that large ship out there rather than giving your sorry arse advice. So listen up, lad. You can woo that young lady back into your arms and be happy for a lifetime or you can be a stubborn old coot like me and let her slip through your fingers to live a lonely life. The choice is yours."

Brianna tossed and turned in her restless sleep. She found herself running through the backfields of the convent in the middle of the night, searching for Shawn in the darkness. His voice jumped out at her, pleading for her to come to him. Frustrated, she searched for him among the flower gardens, along the stone paths, everywhere she could think, but to no avail.

When she found herself standing in the small, dark chapel behind the convent, a motionless body lay by her feet. She turned over the body and screamed out Shawn's name. Someone came up behind her and tried to pull her away from Shawn's body, which only made her more frantic, until she woke up and looked into the deep brown eyes of the only man she loved, the only man she could ever love.

"Brianna, I'm here, lass." When she looked up at him, her eyes dazed, he added, "Ye were screamin' my name in yer sleep."

Brianna blinked, trying to wake fully. "I thought I lost you."

"I'm right here, flesh and bones before ye," Shawn assured.

Suddenly fully awake, she came to her senses and sat straight up in bed. "You're here!"

"Aye, it took me a while, but I tracked the horses into town."

Brianna looked away, uncomfortable. Her mind raced through the possible reasons she could give him for being here.

Shawn lifted her face toward him. "We need to talk." When she didn't say a word, he continued. "I never wanted this month to end."

She looked up confused. "You didn't?"

He took hold of her hands in his and smoothly massaged the chill that still lingered beneath her skin.

"I'm not good with words, Bri." He put up his hand when she was about to disagree. "I mean words not on paper, words that come from my heart. I'll agree with whatever ye want to do tomorrow, but today I must be truthful with ye.

"If ye told me last month that I would be married to a Catholic gil, I would have laughed in yer face, so hilarious an idea it would have seemed to me with my harsh feelings toward that faith. Over the past month, I've learned that the building that ye worship in doesn't make the person. No, what's tucked deep inside yer heart is what's important."

Shawn took a deep breath. "Bri, I know how much gaining the black veil means to ye. So I won't pressure ye to stay with me, but I do have something to tell ye."

"You don't have to do this, Shawn. I know you feel some twisted sense of responsibility towards me, especially since the kidnapping, but I'm okay. There's no need to worry about me any longer."

"Bri, will ye open yer ears and listen to me?"

"I don't want you to feel pressured to say things you don't mean," she stressed, her hands twisting on her lap.

"So it's the black veil ye're still craving then," Shawn replied.

Brianna vehemently shook her head. "All I know is that I'm not going to rely on your charity any longer."

Shawn stood to leave, but Brianna's next words stopped him.

"I never fit in at the convent, and I've come to realize that there was a reason for that – I was never meant to be a nun," she confessed. "I didn't want to lose my home. I knew becoming a nun would make certain that I stayed at the convent forever. I never received a calling from God to become a nun. I realize that now."

Shawn knelt down on a knee in front of her. He stilled her twisting fingers by placing her hands within his own. "Brianna Lawrence, I've been a fool for allowin' ye to think that I only married ye out of obligation. I've loved ye from the first time ye fainted into my arms, whether I knew it then or not. Please give me the chance to make it up to ye. Stay with me for a lifetime, lass, and I promise to make certain not a day goes by that ye doubt my love."

He pulled out the elaborately carved gold band with the aquamarine stone set in its center. The color of the stone reminded him of their day at sea when she risked her life just to be with him. Finding it only an hour ago was a miracle in itself. The merchant's doors were closed because of the storm, but he stated his emergency to the owner and was pleased with the outcome.

"I wanted to do this proper this time to show ye how much I care for ye."

Brianna was overcome with emotion. Tears streamed freely down her face. "You don't have to do this."

He lifted her body off the bed and carried her into the main room of the pub. "Woman, I love you."

Brianna was taken aback by the sight before her. Hundreds of candles, all of them scattered on tables, and along the counter of the bar, lit the room. Flowers surrounded the base of all the candles, their flora filling every space of the pub. If she closed her eyes, she'd imagine she was in a meadow filled with flowers.

She tilted her head up. "You did all this ... for me?"

"With a little help." Shawn nodded toward the men sitting in the dark corners of the pub, all of them careful not to intrude on their moment.

"Forget we're even here," the barkeep replied with a faint smile and small wave.

"Will ye stay married to me, renew our vows before God and all the men at this bar? This time for all the right reasons?" Shawn asked.

The door crashed open with the wind. "Ye didn't think we'd miss another of your weddings, did ye now?" Aunt Bea and Aunt Liddea both chimed as they walked into the pub with Pastor McOliver in tow.

Before Shawn could answer, another group made their way into the pub. When they pushed back their hoods, Brianna screamed with excitement.

"Sister Mary Louise, Sister Mary Clarence, and Father McBrien! You're here, how wonderful to see all of you!"

"Thank your husband for that. He extended an invitation to us to visit." Sister Mary Louise surveyed the room. "It looks like God made sure our timing was perfect."

Pastor McOliver stepped forward.

Shawn nudged Brianna aside. "I'll make certain ye never doubt my love for ye ever again, Bri. Will ye marry me … again?"

Brianna looked into her husband's eyes, remembering the first time their eyes met and held, her heart shaken then as now.

"I will," she said softly, shyly.

He leaned in close, his breath a whisper away, his lips lightly teasing her with a kiss. "I'll also make certain ye're no goin' to faint tonight," he promised with a wink.

That night when he took her into his arms, there was a need to be met, and a marriage long overdue to consummate.

EPILOGUE

Brianna held onto the last note of the song until her breath ran out and the sound of applause vibrated the walls of the church. She heaved a deep, contented sigh, her heart full.

Her eyes searched below the choir loft for her husband among the sea of faces smiling up at her. When she didn't find him sitting in his usual pew, she remembered he was going to visit his mother's grave today, the anniversary of her death.

Tonight, she would give him her good news. It would pull him out of his melancholy mood. Even now, excitement bubbled up inside her at the thought of it.

She glanced out the window toward the cemetery to see two figures lying on the ground beside the gravestones. Instinct had her running through the field beside the church and up the small hill to the cemetery. Her breath caught in her throat at the sight before her.

Shawn's father turned at the sound of his footsteps. His face wet with tears.

"I should have known it'd be you," Francis McBrien stated, his voice quiet, his eyes filled with sadness. With a faint smile, he said, "I've been talking with your mother. Told her what a wonderful man you turned out to be. Wish there had been more time," he began, his knees dropping to the ground beside his mother's grave. His hand clutching his heart.

"Don't talk, there's no need," Shawn stated, falling to his knees beside him. He began to scoop his father's body into his arms. "I'll bring you to the doc."

Francis McBrien shook his head, pushing his hands away. "No, I'll finish my life here with your mother, least I could do."

"Ye're bein' foolish. Let me take ye down the road, jus a short walk. Doc will get ye feelin' better soon enough."

His father's hand gripped his own, stopping him from standing.

157

"Too many years lost, you and I. Wished I had been there for your mother, my only regret," he stated, his voice weak.

"'Tis past and forgiven," Shawn assured.

His father nodded, his face serious. "Go on and be the father I never was. I've a need to be with your mother now."

He watched him slowly close his eyes as he breathed out his last breath.

"No, we're not finished yet, ye and I. Ye can't leave me now. I won't allow it."

He hugged his father's body close, rocking back and forth, struggling to hold back his tears. Regretting the many years lost, focused only on his anger.

A hand lightly squeezed his shoulder. His head tipped back to see his wife's face.

"Shawn, I'm so sorry." Tears streamed down her face. "He was a good man," she choked out.

"I know."

She sat beside her husband, leaning against him, weeping with him. It seemed death strode hand in hand with life. Tonight, she'd tell him a babe grew within her.

*

Printed in the United States
775700001B